you don't love me yet

## also by jonathan lethem

*The Disappointment Artist* (essays)
*Men and Cartoons* (stories)
*The Fortress of Solitude*
*This Shape We're In*
*Motherless Brooklyn*
*Girl in Landscape*
*As She Climbed Across the Table*
*The Wall of the Sky, the Wall of the Eye* (stories)
*Amnesia Moon*
*Gun, with Occasional Music*

## with carter scholz

*Kafka Americana*

## as editor

*The Vintage Book of Amnesia*
*The Year's Best Music Writing 2002*

u don't love me yet you don't love me y

doubleday / new york london toronto sydney auckland

you don't love me yet

JONATHAN LETHEM

PUBLISHED BY DOUBLEDAY

Copyright © 2007 by Jonathan Lethem

Published in the United States by Doubleday, an imprint
of The Doubleday Broadway Publishing Group, a division
of Random House, Inc., New York.
www.doubleday.com

DOUBLEDAY and the portrayal of an anchor with a
dolphin are registered trademarks of Random House, Inc.

*Book design by Jennifer Ann Daddio*

Library of Congress Cataloging-in-Publication Data

Lethem, Jonathan.
  You don't love me yet / Jonathan Lethem.
   p. cm.
   1. Musicians—California—Los Angeles—Fiction. I. Title.
  PS3562.E8544Y68 2007
  813'.54—dc22
                                          2006011768

ISBN-13: 978-0-385-51218-3

PRINTED IN THE UNITED STATES OF AMERICA

10  9  8  7  6  5  4  3  2  1

First Edition

for eliot duhan

*Mistakes are bound to happen, there's gonna be another summer*
*I know what I think and what I'm supposed to do*
*Maybe I don't think as much as you*

—"YOU DON'T LOVE ME YET,"
THE VULGAR BOATMEN

*I have my start*
*But I have never begun*
*Because without you my life is unsung*

—"YOU DON'T LOVE ME YET,"
ROKY ERICKSON

you don't love me yet

# one

**t**hey met at the museum to end it. There, wandering through high barren rooms full of conceptual art, alone on a Thursday afternoon, Lucinda Hoekke and Matthew Plangent felt certain they wouldn't be tempted to do more than talk. Too, driving into the canyon of vacated plazas of downtown Los Angeles felt suitably solemn and irrevocable. The plan was not to sever as friends, or as bandmates, only as lovers.

Lucinda saw him first. A tall, malnourished vegetarian, Matthew was obliviously handsome, lead-singer handsome. He was dressed as for his work at the zoo and for the band's practices, in black turtleneck, jeans, and speckless suede work boots, which Lucinda knew he kept in his locker when he entered the animals' habitats. Matthew had presumably been excused from his veterinary nursing duties for the afternoon, or possibly it was his day off. For the past four years Lucinda had been assembling espresso drinks and clearing dishes at the Coffee Chairs, but she'd quit her job the day before, part of the same program of change that included this final rupture with Matthew. Instead, to pay her rent Lucinda had agreed to work for her friend Falmouth Strand in his storefront gallery.

On her way into the museum Lucinda had paused at two heroic pillars of neon, mounted on either side of a doorway, and seen only versions of herself and Matthew: discrete, sealed, radiant. Now, sighting Matthew, she felt her senses quicken, her balance shifting to her toes. He squinted warily at a television monitor on a white pediment, some sort of video art. Perhaps it was the case that for him, as for her, everything in the museum had been reduced to an allegory of their dilemma. Exhausted by the old tug of his beauty, his scruffy intensity and lean limbs, Lucinda was ready to send Matthew and his allure out voyaging elsewhere.

She joined silently to his side, the tiny hairs of their arms bristling together electrically. The two wandered like zombies through the exhibition, hesitating for a long while at a pair of basketballs floating perfectly suspended at midpoint in a glass water tank.

"The thing is we've done this so much before we're too good at it."

Matthew's gaze remained fixed on the tank. "You mean there's nothing to say."

"Yes, but also we don't believe it's real because we've fallen back together so many times afterward. We need to make a difference between this time and all those others."

"This time we're serious, Lucinda."

"On the other hand, the advantage to so many practice breakups is we know we still like each other, so we don't have to worry that we're not going to be friends."

"Yes."

"The band will be okay."

"Yes."

"If we seem like we're barely speaking to each other Denise and Bedwin will be completely confused. We can't let the band worry about us. Bedwin's fragile enough as it is."

"Yes."

"Is something else wrong?"

"It's nothing. There's a sort of crisis with one of the zoo's kangaroos, that's all."

"You were thinking about a kangaroo just now?"

"I just kind of wish we were in someplace more private so I could hold you and maybe just kiss you a little bit." His dark woeful eyes flitted past her, as if hounded. "I feel like I can't even look at you."

"I feel the same way, but that's the point. We have to stop now, change our patterns."

"I should stop having breakfast at the Coffee Chairs."

"You can go to the Coffee Chairs all you like. I quit yesterday."

"Are you serious?"

"I'm going to work for Falmouth."

Matthew disliked Falmouth. Lucinda and Falmouth had been together, briefly, in college. Matthew had always behaved jealously around Falmouth, though he denied it.

"Work how? Doing what?"

"He offered me a job in a sort of theatrical piece he's putting together. A fake office that needs fake office workers to answer real telephone calls."

"Calls from who?"

"I don't know. A complaint line, he said."

"I don't get it."

"I don't either, yet. But Falmouth will make it clear. Speaking of which, he has a piece in here somewhere, he showed me once."

"Is that why we're here? Is this about Falmouth?"

"What are you talking about?"

"Are you trying to tell me you're going to be with Falmouth now?"

"I could never be with Falmouth again. You know me better than that. He isn't even going to be at the gallery most of the time, that's why he needs to hire me. Come on, this way."

She dragged him by the hand, through impoverished galleries, white rooms barely ornamented apart from seven tiny pyramids of wheat germ.

"Here, this is Falmouth's thing."

Falmouth's object had been plopped ingloriously in the middle of an atrium, seemingly exiled. A white crate or cube. Matthew circled it skeptically.

"This white box is everything I can't stand about contemporary everything."

"No, wait, see, it's not a box."

Matthew read aloud the artwork's identifying label, on the opposite wall. *"Chamber Containing the Volumetric Representation of the Number of Hours It Took Me to Arrive at This Idea, Mixed Media, 1988."*

"It has a door, look."

"I don't know if you're supposed to—"

"Falmouth built it, don't worry."

"Hey, it's a little room."

"See, why would all this stuff be in here if we weren't meant to see it?"

"It's just like Falmouth to hide the good part."

"I wonder if there's anything to drink in that refrigerator."

"It would have to be like airplane drinks, little bottles."

"Let's find out."

Matthew touched her at the waist and guided her through the low entrance to the chamber. "Hurry," he said, "before anyone comes."

Inside, she crouched, seated herself on the sled-size bed. Then took Matthew's hand and tugged him onto her lap. "Close the door, quick." She slid her hand along his hip, to the waist of his thready, pale-bleached jeans. He wore no underwear. His smooth belly flinched to concavity under her fingertips.

"Wait—"

"Kiss me."

"Does this door lock?"

"Who cares, no one's here, we're the only ones in the whole museum."

Lucinda braced against the tiny bedposts as Matthew wrinkled her jeans over her knees. The refrigerator slid to the room's corner as she batted it with her toes, but there was nowhere else to put her leg. Matthew arched low to keep from topping against the room's ceiling. Lucinda kissed his craning neck.

"The last time," she managed.

"Of course."

"For real, it has to be for real."

"It is for real."

"The band, we can't mess up the band—"

"We won't, they won't know the difference, it'll just be you and me as friends and the band will be fine."

"Just friends now, Matthew—"

"Yes—"

# two

**t**here's a certain kind of talk I have with women," the voice complained. "I say whatever I'm thinking about love and sex and blah, blah, blah, I've heard myself a thousand times. But as normal as it is for me—this kind of frank talk, I mean—for women it seems like it's always the first time in their lives they've ever spoken that way."

"There's nothing so strange in that," Lucinda suggested. "You're accustomed to yourself, but you surprise others."

"Surprise would be one thing," said the complainer. "But I

*change* others. I affect people. Women. Something happens to them, but nothing happens to me. The sameness of my life is confirmed by the effect I have on women. They're always changed. Maybe if I met somebody who wasn't surprised by me something new would happen."

"You mean falling in love?" Perhaps the caller was only some dreary seducer, impressed with his own unresponsiveness.

"Oh, I've fallen in love."

Lucinda adjusted the telephone on her shoulder and craned sideways to peer beyond the edge of the cubicle. Falmouth wasn't at the storefront gallery's reception desk. She caught scent of his coffee pot, dregs charring to a shrill odor. Vehicles coursed outside. At four in the afternoon the sun on Sunset Boulevard was as pale and flinty as morning light. Cubicles at either side of Lucinda sat empty. The office was little more than library carrels that Falmouth's carpenters had slapped together, then painted gray.

The yellow legal pad before Lucinda lay bare. She raised her pen and mimed script in the air. "Tell me," she said.

"Look," he said, "I fall in love every five minutes. I might be half in love with you now."

"You're not the first caller to this line to say that," she said.

"Love is everywhere."

"I'm supposed to be writing down your complaints," she reminded him.

"Okay, right," he said. "Well, today's complaint can be about what happens when I fall in love. Though I try not to, anymore. It makes me bad at being where I am."

"I don't understand."

"If I really fell in love with you, then when we hung up the phone I'd be stuck halfway. I'd be all disjointed in time and space, half there and half here. And I don't even know where there *is*. Whereas now, we get off the phone, no trouble. I'm where I am, like the Buddhists prefer."

"We all want to keep the Buddhists happy."

"The little Buddhists inside of ourselves, those are the ones I worry about."

"But you still haven't really told me what happens when you really fall in love," she said. "Only that you want to avoid it."

"My eyes destroy you."

"What?"

"I have this condition called monster eyes. I find something not to like and it becomes enormous, it becomes the whole world. Once it was a woman's fingernails. I started to think they were too weird and short and stubby, and then it was all I could think about. I tried encouraging her to work on her cuticles, to push them up—am I disgusting you?"

"No."

"I told myself that if she'd just work on her hands I'd go back to adoring her. But really there were other things about her voice and personality and the way she fucked that were waiting to take the place of the fingernails. I'd begun to erode and degrade her in my mind. With my monster eyes."

Cradling the pen at the point like chalk, Lucinda wrote, in block letters, M-O-N-S-T-E-R E-Y-E-S.

"So," he continued, "sometimes I think the kindest thing I can do for a person is keep them out of range of those eyes. Like keeping a wolf out of moonlight."

"You mean a wolfman," Lucinda corrected.

"Well if he isn't exposed to the moon it doesn't have to get to that point."

"But isn't a wolfman a man before he sees the moon? Rather than a wolf? But anyway, the danger in a wolfman seeing the moon isn't to the wolfman—"

"Or the moon."

Stymied, Lucinda drew a rudimentary wolfman on the pad: a smiley face fringed with snaky hairs. What seemed hippieish sideburns gained a fiercer cast as she scribbled them nearly to the eyes.

"The thing about a wolfman is that something repulsive emerges from hiding," said Lucinda. "But that isn't the fault of the person who sees it. Maybe she just had ugly hands—"

Turning, Lucinda found Falmouth scowling over her shoulder at the block letters and pie-faced wolfman on the canary pad. Where had he been lurking? Falmouth turned his wrist to show Lucinda his watch, then pointed to the phone, where a square red button of translucent plastic blinked. Another complaint, waiting to be recorded. She shrugged guiltily.

"I'm sorry, sir, our time is up," she told the caller.

"Tell me your name," said the complainer.

"You know I can't do that, sir."

"Okay, I'll call again tomorrow."

"That's your prerogative," she said into the phone. It was one of the generic replies Falmouth had originally scripted for her and the other complaint receptionists. She hung up before he could reply, and took the next call.

———

**W**ho were you talking to when I came in?"

"Who do you think? A complainer."

"It sounded like you knew him."

"He had a lot to say." It wasn't a lie. He'd had a lot to say the day before, too. That he'd called each day of the past week Lucinda left unmentioned.

Lucinda and Falmouth sat in white plastic chairs at the edge of Sunset Boulevard's sidewalk, under the shade of the Siete Mares patio. Falmouth faced west, squinting in the declining April sun. They'd departed the Strand Gallery for an early dinner, after the arrival of Falmouth's two interns to man the complaint lines. Falmouth had culled the spookily young and confident interns from his students at CalArts, where he taught a class on installation art. At his gallery, a showcase solely for his own spectacles, Falmouth employed only women. Soon Falmouth would need more than three of them. The frequency of calls had mushroomed as word spread through Los Angeles, by means of bright orange stickers reading "Complaints? Call 213 291 7778," mounted on public telephones, also by the interns, in restaurants, cocktail bars, and hotel lobbies.

Two ruined plates of fish tacos lay before them, the table covered with shreds of spilled cabbage and dots of red sauce and sour cream. Falmouth, though, sat unstained and impeccable in his trim brown sharkskin suit and vintage tie. He'd begun wearing tailored suits, polished shoes, and silk ties during his and Lucinda's last year of college. The rest of their friends wore T-shirts and jeans, then and now. The suits debuted at the same time Falmouth had begun to lose his hair. Lucinda recalled poignantly the wisps that had wreathed Falmouth's ears and neck, overlapping his collars, even as the bareness on top expanded, naked, undeniable, silly. Lucinda and Falmouth's affair had been finished just before he began shaving his dome clean. Falmouth's first and most successful piece of art was himself, installed in the larger gallery of the world.

"Don't lose control of the dialogues, Lucinda," Falmouth said. "You can't begin thinking the complaint line is somehow a real service. The *Echo Park Annoyance* is coming tomorrow for an interview. We ought to seem institutional. As though we're recording these complaints for some scientific or altruistic purpose, yet couldn't care less about the yearnings of any given caller. It's not a hipster chat line."

Lucinda recognized Falmouth's jabber as a symptom. "You're nervous about this interview."

"Be dispassionate," he said, dismissing her sympathy. "This piece needs to have a certain gloss."

"Some men find it erotic to talk to a woman on the telephone, Falmouth. You underestimated the titillation effect. I get breathers."

"You're mistaken. I had titillation in mind. When you take a complaint you ought to sound like a beautiful nurse. Patient but slightly bored. As if you're wearing a uniform that you'll remove only after the conversation, not during. As if your real life is elsewhere." Falmouth turned and bugged his eyes at an old woman laden with shopping bags who paused on the sidewalk, overhearing him. The woman shook her head and resumed plodding. Falmouth motioned with cupped hands, as if scooting the woman along the sidewalk by the buttocks.

"Maybe then you should have hired someone who had a real life elsewhere," said Lucinda.

"Has it never been explained to you that self-pity under-mines sarcasm? Pick one or the other, then stick with it."

Lucinda daubed at her stained plate, scooping fallen shreds of fish and cabbage, slurping from her fingers. Falmouth sighed, radiating disappointment that Lucinda wouldn't tangle with him.

"Falmouth, when you and I were together, were you in love with me?"

He winced. "I suppose I was. It appeared so at the time, didn't it? Do you want a cigarette?"

"Maybe you only seemed to be in love. Suppose, appear, seem, I hate those words."

"Why are we discussing this now?"

"Nothing, it's just someday I want to be in love without sup-posing or appearing or seeming."

"You want to be in love? Or you want somebody to be in love with you? It can't be both, that's like mingling self-pity and sar-casm. What's the latest development with Matthew?"

Sunset gloom had overtaken the boulevard. Falmouth looked tired. He was anxious about the complaint piece. And older. They were all getting older.

"We've broken up," Lucinda said. "I'll see him tonight, at practice."

"So you're friends."

"Matthew's too mild to be anybody's enemy. And we refuse to wreck the band. So instead we're miserable."

"Voilà. It's love."

"I want real true clear passion, not murk and misery."

"You underestimate the value of your inertia and dismay."

Falmouth had been slumbering, coasting through the talk. Now his attention gelled. "Misery's much better than happiness. It's auspicious that you're in a band together."

"Just because we're as unhappy as a great rock band doesn't mean we don't suck."

"You're being too hard on yourselves. Most great rock bands are not only unhappy, they also suck, if you listen closely enough."

"You never knew anything about music, Falmouth."

"No, I never did. Don't you want a cigarette?"

the band barely fit into its rehearsal space, formerly the living room of drummer Denise Urban, now with its floor triply carpeted and bay windows draped with a bedspread to insulate the band's sounds from irritated neighbors. Denise, muscular and nearly breastless in a scant white T-shirt, blue eyes half covered by her high hennaed bangs, balanced on a stool crammed between her kit and the French doors to her bedroom. On a couch of threadbare gingham, beneath bookshelves drooping on their brackets, sat Bedwin Greenish, the band's lead guitarist, lyricist, and arranger. Bedwin wore plaid shirts buttoned to his throat, and cut his hair himself, with children's scissors. He sat coiled around his black electric guitar, corduroyed legs tangled in themselves, one sneakered foot bobbing, head dipped so that his glasses neared his fingers, which spidered on the guitar's fretwork noiselessly.

Matthew stood at the room's center, leaning on his microphone stand with his back to the drums, acoustic guitar strapped across his shoulder but dangling untouched. Matthew knew only rudimentary chords, his strumming inessential to the band's sound. He turned and stared unhelpfully while Lucinda, arriving last, wrestled her enormous hard case through the kitchen doorway. The room was silent enough to hear Bedwin throat-humming the notes of an imaginary solo.

"Hey," said Lucinda.

"Hey," said Denise.

"Um?" said Bedwin.

Matthew nodded as Lucinda fitted herself into her accustomed spot at his left elbow. A bass player's stance, pivot between drummer and singer, the only player to absorb everyone's reactions. She'd face Bedwin too, if he ever looked up. But it was Matthew's presence to which she attuned now, his delicate eyes so firmly unglanced in her direction. She felt a kind of heat impression of his contour glow along the side of her body that was turned toward his.

The sensation, pleasant or unpleasant, was familiar enough to ignore. She plugged in and tuned her strings. "Somebody give me a G."

Bedwin plucked a note, unamplified, then turned himself up and plucked it again. Denise rattled her snare warningly. Matthew coughed.

Lucinda boinged her ill-tuned string, but her ear failed her. "Sorry, another G?" Matthew and Bedwin each replied with their guitars. This time she nailed it.

"So, Bedwin's got something new he wants to try," said Matthew, still not looking at anyone in particular.

"Great," said Lucinda. Bedwin himself didn't seem to register the discussion, his glasses still magnetized to the guitar's neck.

"Sure, but let's do a run-through first," said Denise. The

heartbeat of their music, she was also the conscience of the band's claim to professionalism. They hadn't practiced in ten days. So, the four shrugged halfway through their set list: "Shitty Citizen," "Temporary Feeling," "The Houseguest," and "Hell Is for Buildings." Then worked a few times over the ending to "Canary in a Coke Machine," struggling with the elusive full-stop timing. The band possessed these five songs, and five more. It was enough to make a set which, crisply played, lasted thirty-five minutes. A credible duration, if you relied on between-song patter and false starts, plus a break after "Sarah Valentine" and, you'd have to hope, a round of applause calling them back to the stage to finish with "Secondhand Apologies." Credible, except the band was sick of "Crayon Fever" and "Temporary Feeling." The oldest songs in their set, both felt embarrassing and slight. They all rooted for Bedwin to write more songs. He hadn't in a while. Not that anyone meant to start panicking about it.

Lucinda adored thumping the fat strings of her instrument, constructing with the stretched notes a physical bridge between Denise's peppery beat and Bedwin's chords, a bridge across which Matthew's voice could scurry or shamble or cavort. She felt she ought to hide her secret passion for rehearsal, the uncommon extent of pleasure she felt in simply generating the same figures over and over, those low, mumbling bass lines Bedwin had scripted with her capacities in mind. She wasn't the fastest, but she'd been assured by better players that she possessed all anyone needed: She swung. She had feel. Lucinda took solace in these notions without comprehending them fully. Bass players were a secret guild, each abiding with the ungainly, disrespected instrument for the thankless benefit of music itself. Lucinda had read somewhere of the argument as to who derived the most pleasure from the sexual act, the male or the female. She felt certain the musical reply would be: the bass player.

Halfway through teaching the band his new song—he'd stepped to the drums and quickly set a rhythm figure for Denise to play, shown Lucinda a bass line by playing it on the upper two strings of his guitar, then strummed chords for Matthew to follow—Bedwin seemed to lapse into glazed discouragement at his spot on the gingham cushions. The song was sprightly and appealing, its changes easy to remember and play, and the band cycled through several choruses hopefully, waiting for Bedwin to further enlighten them. But rather than suppling lead lines on his guitar or offering Matthew a lyric, he fell to silence, then issued a faint moan. The players ground to an incongruent halt.

"Hey, Bedwin," said Matthew. "You okay?"

"Sure . . . sorry . . ."

"Bedwin," said Denise, more sharply. "Did you eat anything today?"

"Um, sure, yeah."

"Tell me what you ate."

"I, uh, definitely had some raisin bran."

"I mean any dinner or anything, Bedwin. Before coming to rehearsal."

"I can't tell you exactly when it was," he mumbled defiantly.

Sighing, Denise slid from behind her drums. "I bought some groceries today, all the stuff you like. How about some ginger ale and a baloney sandwich? I got some beer, too, if anyone wants one."

Bedwin shifted his guitar to one side, expending minimum effort in freeing himself from its weight, then ambled behind Denise into the kitchen. Lucinda and Matthew were left alone.

Matthew ducked his head under his guitar strap and parked his instrument against an amp. Lucinda unloaded her bass. Accompanied by the faint music of Denise's refrigerator, which began chortling and whining the moment its door was opened, and the tinkering of a blade in jars of mustard and mayonnaise, the two moved to the empty cushions. The ramshackle couch saddled obligingly, dipping their bodies into contact at elbow and shoulder.

"I'm in trouble," said Matthew.

"What trouble?"

"I quit on Tuesday. Dr. Marian was so pissed she won't even let me into my locker. Shelf is dying of ennui and nobody will admit it."

"Who's Shelf?"

"The kangaroo. You remember."

Lucinda and Matthew had sworn not to speak on the telephone. The ten days since their breakup had passed without those chance encounters for which, heart tripping, she'd braced at the entry to each of his regular haunts, the Back Door Bakery, Hard Times Pizza, Netty's. Their abandoned intimacy dwelled like a rumor between them, independent and charged.

Lucinda put her hand into Matthew's hair. He leaned his skull into her hand. Lucinda spotted a tiny nesting of dandruff grains in the blazing red cup of his ear, as usual.

"You'll be back in a week," she said.

"I don't know this time."

"Did you leave something important in your locker?"

"More I'm worried about Shelf."

"Shelf's probably just a little depressed."

"Shelf's fucking inconsolable."

"You see aspects of yourself in the kangaroo," Lucinda said gently. "But you're not dying."

"I might be suffocating slowly, who knows, it's hard to tell. Like all of us. We're turning thirty and we haven't done anything. Look at Bedwin. He can't even feed himself, and he's our genius."

"The song's good."

"It's not a song yet," said Matthew. "He hasn't got any lyrics, he told me."

Inside the kitchen, Bedwin choked, wolfing his food. A kettle rattled on its burner. Denise went on puttering at the stove and refrigerator, allowing them privacy.

"Anyone can write lyrics," suggested Lucinda.

"Anyone can be in a lame band, anyone can scoop up the hair shed by a depressed molting kangaroo, anyone can wipe the tears from the infected eyes of a bandicoot, anyone can put a monkey in handcuffs," said Matthew savagely. "For that matter, anyone can answer telephones in fucking Falmouth's stupid pretend gallery, or work in a porn store—"

"Denise doesn't work in a porn store," whispered Lucinda. "Keep your voice down."

"Masturbation boutique, whatever it is."

Lucinda saw she'd roiled Matthew by touching his hair, by breaching the distance. If he'd been the one to speak consolingly she'd surely now be in his role. Abjection and solace switched between them as lightly and easily as electric current.

"Bedwin's the only one of us who actually lives for his art," said Matthew, more evenly. "And see where it gets him."

"Maybe you really should quit the zoo."

"I can't abandon Shelf."

"Is Shelf a male or a female kangaroo?"

"A flyer."

"What's a flyer?" Lucinda, suddenly in the grip of an absurd jealousy, felt certain she knew the answer.

"That's the word for a female. A lady kangaroo."

"Of course," she said bitterly.

Denise and Bedwin emerged from the kitchen. Matthew and Lucinda fumbled apart on the couch.

"What about one of those beers?" said Lucinda.

"Sure." Denise grabbed one from the fridge. Lucinda twisted off the beer's cap and pulled a long sip from its neck. Matthew frowned, turned his back to the band. They reclaimed their instruments and, at Denise's prompting, encored "Tree of Death," probably their favorite among their songs if they were honest with themselves. Bedwin, restored by the sandwich, managed a plinking, gnarled solo. Matthew lowered his voice to a whisper during the bridge, seducing an audience that wasn't there.

Outside, a moonless night had fallen on the terraced apartments of Landa Street and Kenilworth Avenue, shadow swarming the concrete steps, bushed with jade plants, that wended up from the silence of parked cars, so distant from the blacktop heat and scurry of wheels on Silver Lake and Hyperion. Beyond the band's windows something four-footed crashed in the under leaves, daring itself to raid Denise's garbage bin. Inside, the quartet was complete for one instant, rollicking in the embrace of the sound they produced themselves, free from time and hesitation. If only it could go on forever. Bedwin wrote short songs.

The band didn't have a name yet, though they'd discussed it hundreds of times.

The whatever-it-was got into the garbage, whining as it ravaged a foil-lined takeaway bag.

"Let's play the new one," said Lucinda, after the band stuttered to silence. "I can't get it out of my head." She slugged the last of her beer, went to the fridge and found another.

"I already told Matthew and Denise," said Bedwin. "I really don't have any lyrics."

"No problem," said Lucinda, wiping her mouth. "You'll write some." She set the new bottle at the base of her amp and retook her place, expectantly.

"I've been trying. I'm having a sort of problem with language."

"What do you mean?"

"With sentences . . . words."

"We know what language is, Bedwin," said Denise, not unkindly.

The three had turned to Bedwin now, half consciously, as though reaching out to support someone freshly released from a hospital, a man tapping down a ramp on crutches.

"My problem is I don't believe in the place where the sentences come from anymore."

"Lucinda says anyone can write lyrics," said Matthew.

"Go to hell," said Lucinda. "Let's just play it. I'll make up some words, sure."

"I didn't mean—" began Matthew.

"No, you're absolutely right," said Lucinda. "Pick up your guitar."

Lucinda plumped at her bass strings, jump-starting the song, and planted her thighs in a new stance, facing Denise, demanding the drums' reply. Denise met the call, ticked the beat double-time. The sound was sprung, uncanny, preverbal, the bass and drum the rudiment of life itself, argument and taunt, and each turn of the figure a kiss-off until the cluster of notes began again. Who needed words? Who even needed guitars, those preening whiners? Lucinda felt violently unapologetic. And when the guitars wended in she wasn't any sorrier. Meeting Lucinda's challenge had stirred even Bedwin, who now confessed with his lead line that the wordless song had a melodic hook.

Denise sped up and no one cared.

The thing that rooted in garbage heard them. It dropped the chicken carcass it had plucked from the foil bag and bayed its own song into the tops of the trees.

"Monster eyes," Lucinda called out at the peak of the chorus. The others turned and gaped.

"Get you out of range of my monster eyes," she sang atonally at the chorus's reprise. "Best thing I ever did for you, was get you out of range of my monster eyes—"

Then she fumbled her way into the verse's start: "Before my eyes destroy you, better run, better run—" She hummed to dummy another line: "Nuh nuh huh feel my eyes abhor you, dunna nuh, dunna nuh—"

Matthew, not looking at Lucinda, grabbed the lyric at the next pass. He pigeoned his toes and shouted it at the draped windows as if to press it out into the night, then dropped register, incanting the lyric as a warning instead, his hair falling forward, gorgeously, into his eyes. Bedwin nodded. He quit playing lead fills in favor of the raw chord changes, chiming the riff on the downbeat. Denise thwacked her cymbal incontinently, railing above the sound the band was making. The words were freighted with a righteousness and panic each player felt as a confession. A voicing they couldn't have sanctioned alone, only collectively. They chanted it in murmurs together the next time through, the now-already-inevitable chorus, inseparable from Bedwin's chords:

*Get you*
*out of range*
*of my*
*monster*
*eyes—*

Their hearts huddled around the fledgling song as if it were a tendril of bonfire in wild darkness, something they nurtured which fed them in return.

Lucinda, in shorts and sleeveless top, stretched in her chair in front of Millie's Café, shading her eyes with one bare arm. Coffee steamed untouched on the table, too hot for the day. Noon light had drawn her to the sidewalk table like a snake lured to bathing on rock. Sporadic pedestrians blobbed past on their shadow forms. Los Angeles was a desert. The cars on Sunset Boulevard felt miles away across the margin of curb, tumbleweeds scouring paths to nowhere.

Deep in the luxury of Lucinda's trance an alarm sounded. She lifted her arm from her eyes. A small man in black horn-rimmed glasses and a backward baseball cap had silently leaned to fit his face into her armpit, his nose nearly brushing her sprig of hair, his lips and eyelids narrowed in an expression of savor.

The man, perhaps fifty, wore a wrinkled suit jacket over a gray T-shirt, with jeans and sneakers. He hopped back as she shifted, as though she'd startled him. She supposed she had. He had an abrupt flustered quality, like a woken duck.

"How do you do," he said, righting himself. "The way you were sitting was extraordinarily lovely. I hope I didn't disturb you."

"Well, you did."

"Then I regret it. Jules Harvey." He offered his hand, which she took unthinkingly.

"Luc—" she began, then stopped, dropping his hand.

"Luce? I wonder if you could tell me where to find Maltman Avenue."

Lucinda's tattooed waitress edged to her table, slipping the check beneath a saucer.

"Maltman's the next block." Lucinda pointed. "Look, you shouldn't do that." She slurped her tepid coffee, worthless now. It should have been iced.

"You mean—"

"Sneak up on people," she said. She didn't want to hear what he'd call it.

"I know, I know." He pursed his lips, weighing the indulgence. At last he sighed, seeming to find it in himself to forgive. He fished in his jacket's interior pocket for a folding map. "Have you heard of the Falmouth Strand Gallery?"

She walked Jules Harvey to the gallery's entrance, a precinct of chaos. The *Annoyance*'s photographer, a hulking blond in a leather jacket, slugged shoulder-loads of equipment from his double-parked van in through the doorway. Just inside, Falmouth presided, gesticulating furiously. Explaining some point to the *Annoyance*'s writer, whose nodding dreadlocks shrouded the steno pad on which he jotted Falmouth's words.

"Jules," said Falmouth, interrupting himself when they walked through the door. "I'm thrilled to see you. We're a bit of a mess. You met Lucinda, I see." He bugged his eyes at Lucinda, a glare of panic reserved solely for her sake.

Jules Harvey nodded, his expression serene. Perhaps to him the episode on the sidewalk was a reasonable prelude to introduction. He dithered his hands, peering into the gallery's dimmed recesses. "I'll just have a look . . . there's no hurry . . ."

"Lucinda can show you the complaint office."

Jules Harvey trailed Lucinda into the small maze of carrels. One of Falmouth's interns, seated in her cubicle, waved her pen in greeting, then frowned back to her call. On the canary pad before her she'd scrawled: *nobody ever told me about aging/moisturizer/death.* Lights on Lucinda's phone blinked, another three complainers waiting. Now they called in the morning, too. Falmouth's genius or folly, whichever it was, had slowly expanded to swallow Los Angeles.

"Wait in there," Lucinda told Jules Harvey, nodding at another empty cubicle. "You can listen, just don't pick up the phone."

"Sure." Harvey adjusted his black glasses frames and took the seat, meek as a clam. Lucinda had to remind herself he'd invaded her periphery, robbed her private smells.

"Complaints," she said into the phone.

"Say something so I know it's you," said the voice she recognized.

Lucinda had to catch her breath. "We'd be happy to register any dissatisfaction you've experienced, sir."

"I had to hang up on that other girl three times," the caller said.

"There's no need for that now, sir."

"Yes, I can hear it's you."

"Yes."

None of the other complainers interested Lucinda at all. They'd roused her curiosity for the first days, a week at most. After ten days she felt herself turning into a recording instrument. The complainers spoke of their husbands and wives and lovers and children, from cubicles of their own they whispered their despair at being employed, they called to disparage the quality of restaurants and hotels and limousines, they whined of difficulties moving their bowels or persuading anyone to read their screenplays or poetry. They fished for her sympathy. Using Falmouth's scripted lines she dealt with them crisply, addressing them as ma'am and sir, cutting them off before they'd become familiar. The only one that mattered was the brilliant complainer, who interested her entirely too much. His words were like a pulse detected in a vast dead carcass. They seemed born as he spoke them, blooming in the secret space between his voice and Lucinda's ears.

"Here's the thing," he said. "I've been thinking about it since we hung up. When I was younger I used to love women's bodies. I'd drive myself crazy picturing them. It was like women themselves were just the keepers of these glorious animals I wanted to pet. I kept trying to push them out of the way so I could get to this agenda I had with their, you know—flesh."

Lucinda was grateful now for the gallery's infestation by the journalists. Falmouth would be kept at bay. If only there hadn't been an armpit sniffer one cubicle away. She hoped Jules Harvey was listening to the intern's calls, not her own. Lucinda could hear the intern murmuring assent into her receiver, her pen scribbling noisily, filling the pages of legal pads with accounts of complaint, as Falmouth required.

"Later," the complainer went on, "I realized it wasn't women's bodies I loved, it was women, actual women. I know that doesn't seem like much of an accomplishment. But women became my actual friends."

"That doesn't sound like a problem," whispered Lucinda.

"For a while it wasn't. For a while I was happy to have sex with the bodies of my friends. But eventually it wore me down. I couldn't remember what I loved about the bodies because I'd become too fond of the women. It was like a vicious triangle."

Jules Harvey's baseball cap and gleaming lenses rose on the horizon of her carrel. Lucinda turned away, pretended she hadn't noticed. Thinking of Falmouth's imperative, she blurted: "What exactly is your complaint, sir?"

"Same as always," said the complainer. "Nostalgia, except it's not just regular nostalgia. More like nostalgia vu. Longing for longing, instead of for the thing in question."

Lucinda printed L-O-N-G-I-N-G, shielding the pad from view with her shoulder. When she turned, however, she saw Jules Harvey padding in his high-tops through the doorway, through the gallery front.

"Women's bodies don't interest you anymore?" she asked. She instantly regretted a question which sounded too interested.

"I can't even think about women's bodies clearly now, that's what I'm trying to explain. All I can think about is particular women. Their faces, their words. The bodies are totally eclipsed. It's like I can't see the sun anymore. I used to have a sense of purpose in life."

"A guy stuck his face in my armpit a few minutes ago," she whispered. "A total stranger, at a restaurant."

"Why didn't you tell me sooner?"

"I'm in shock, I guess. He crept up while I was sitting with my eyes closed."

"See, there's a person with priorities."

"I don't think he's much of a person at all."

"I bet you he's a leader in his field. Those types thrive in the modern world."

"He's not as assertive as you're imagining. He drifts around like a human dandelion. I should have knocked his block off, but he's too sad-looking."

"Now you're making me jealous. I'm sure I'm twice as sad-looking as your dandelion man—"

Falmouth and the journalist swept into the maze of cubicles, Falmouth babbling in a continuous stream, alive to his imagined public. The photographer orbited, snapping with a tiny camera in his meaty paws.

"Can I call you later?" Lucinda whispered.

"What?"

"Give me your number. I can't talk now."

"Is that a good idea?"

"I'll explain later. I have to start taking complaints."

"I thought that's what we were doing."

"Yes, but—"

"I'll call you," he said, and hung up.

⎯⎯⎯⎯

Lucinda strode Sunset Boulevard, past her own parked Datsun, feeling jubilant and deranged. Men in cars slowed to examine her, a rare walker, but Lucinda didn't turn her head. The sidewalk bowled beneath her like a gerbil's wheel, the city curling to meet her footfalls. A Jeep trolled past with a bumper sticker she'd never seen before, reading POUR LOVE ON THE BROKEN PLACES. The rippled April heat dispelled the cloistered atmosphere of Falmouth's gallery.

The job was worse than her last, making cappuccinos at the Coffee Chairs. It robbed her of a solitude she hadn't known she'd craved until now, the peace achieved performing some simple purpose adequately, in full view of the public but with her dignity and mystery intact. Operating the blistering, groaning espresso machine—thumping out plugs of steam-soaked coffee and tamping fresh grind in its place, venting the pressured steam through the valves in controlled bursts, flash-toweling grit from the joints and threads before burning your fingers—was like playing bass, an anonymous service full of secret satisfaction at precision, clarity, tempo. And it brought her a version of fame. She watched the café's customers recognize her everywhere she went, but declined their glances. Falmouth's callers, by comparison, tugged at her private self, blotted at her with their egos.

Falmouth would be lucky if some museum purchased his lunatic archive of woe and stored it in its basement, there to rot. Complaint was a tide, a drab surf rinsing up everywhere, and by declaring his project Falmouth had drawn the tide to his door. But the complaints existed before Falmouth, and they'd go on after. No one should be forced to listen to them. She couldn't be paid enough. Let Falmouth take the calls himself: that's what Lucinda would have liked to tell the reporter from the *Annoyance*. That was her complaint. Why hadn't the brilliant complainer offered her his number? He didn't sound like anyone's husband. Lucinda saw how little she'd visualized him at all. He was the murmur in her ear, nothing else. Had she ruined things, become too intimate in asking to call? Shouldn't that be what he wanted?

Lucinda's fugue carried her through the doors of No Shame, past a few studious browsers at long shelves of rubber prosthetics and electronic implements, vials of frictionless liquids, and chic racks of videos, with their florid, meaty artwork, to the counter.

"Is Denise here?"

The woman beside the cash register pointed Lucinda to a half-open door. "On break."

Lucinda leaned into a storeroom heaped with cartons, through a doorway decorated like a shrine with thumbtacked Polaroids of unhappy male faces. Denise sat in a wooden folding chair with an unwrapped sandwich on a carton in front of her, sneakers planted in a desert of foam peanuts.

"What's up?" said Denise.

"Falmouth's driving me crazy." Lucinda didn't mention the man whose name she didn't know. The air in the storeroom was heavy, the boxes crammed with erotic supplies too abject to contemplate. Lucinda, perspiring, felt a pleasurable twitching in her calves and realized with what force she'd barreled down Sunset. She ran her fingers down the row of Polaroid mugs. "Who are these?"

"The shit list. When we catch a shoplifter we take their picture. Or anyone else we don't want coming back."

Lucinda looked for Jules Harvey, but he wasn't included.

"It's dead today," said Denise. "They don't need me. Grab a seat."

"I've been in a dimly lit storefront all morning. Can we go get a beer?"

"Just let me wolf this sandwich."

"I've got an even better idea. Let's go to the zoo."

Denise widened her eyes. "You want to see Matthew?"

"They fired him. That's why it's a good time to go. We can look at the animals."

"Okay."

Lucinda riffled the Polaroids again. "You keep the camera here?"

Denise pointed to a cabinet.

"Let's take it along."

t he majority of Los Angeles's kangaroos reclined in a gaggle under tree shade on a tan, scrubby hill. Shelf the Flyer, ostracized instead in a concrete pit, sprawled on her back in desultory glamour, displaying piebald stomach, one leg cocked to the sky in a forlorn show of submission to no one in particular. The pavement of her angled asylum was stained here and there with pissy or vomity streaks, the floor scattered with sun-blanched tatters of uneaten salad. Lucinda, gripping the Polaroid camera, tilted her body as far as she could over the rim of the enclosure and snapped Shelf's portrait. The camera obediently chugged out its product. Lucinda unsheathed the pregnant black square and wagged it in the dry air.

"I can't get that song out of my head," said Denise.

"What song?"

"You know, 'Monster Eyes.' "

"What about it?"

"I don't know, the tune, the riff, the words, whole thing. Bedwin's more unstable these days, but more of a genius, too."

"Yeah," Lucinda admitted. "It's really good."

The zoo was a maze of circular trails disordered by construction, paths barred by scaffolding, displays shielded with plywood. The visible animals seemed to stand off-kilter on their portion of raw-scraped land, their outcroppings. A ram with an erection tiptoed the sculpted ridge of an artificial mountaintop, pacing a ewe who darted on the flip side of their finite mental kingdom. Monkeys dripped from distant palms, more fruit than creature, refusing to dance. A coyote exasperated the limits of his cage, sniffing distance from hills he might have known. Turtles pedaled in dust. The zoo was an abrasion, Los Angeles's arid skeleton poking into evidence.

Lucinda pocketed her snapshot and they walked, searching for the smaller birds and lizards, the depressed little poems veiled in foliage.

"The band's horoscope today said 'a new venture or long-range goal will be given a shot of confidence,' " said Denise. "I think it meant the new song."

"The band's horoscope?"

"I read it every week. The band was born on February sixteenth."

"We're more fetal, I think," said Lucinda. "We need to play a gig. And we need a name."

"We need more good songs," said Denise.

"We have good songs. 'Hell Is for Buildings' sounded great last night."

"We need more. And 'Canary in a Coke Machine' needs a better ending. Also, Bedwin needs to learn to stand up while he plays. He can't sit when we're onstage."

"Maybe we could get him a really high chair. That might be weird."

"Maybe you could write new lyrics to 'Sarah Valentine,' " mused Denise. "Maybe the problem is the lyrics."

"Who is Sarah Valentine anyway? It's sort of a cursed song."

"I think Bedwin went out with a Sarah once for about five minutes."

"I didn't realize Bedwin could shake hands in five minutes. I thought he was more the pining-unspoken-for-years type. I always assumed Sarah was someone who didn't know there was a song about her."

"Matthew looks good, though," said Denise. "He's getting more like a real lead singer."

"What do you mean, like a real singer?"

"Just much sexier and more relaxed, the way he stands at the microphone with his toes pointed and slurs the words, like he can barely be bothered to pronounce the consonants. Like how he sang the new song. You know what I'm talking about."

Lucinda didn't speak. Panting from their ascent to the monkey terraces they quit walking, parked in front of a lemur with cartoon-hobo eyes.

"Do you think Matthew is happy in the band?" said Denise.

"I think he's depressed," said Lucinda irritably. "I think his life is practically falling apart."

"Really? He seemed okay to me."

"He's terrible, terrible."

"Do you think he'll leave the band?"

"Never. We're all he has."

"What about you?"

"I love the band. The band is fine. It's even better now that Matthew and I have broken up. A lot of the great rock-and-roll bands are founded in breakups, love triangles, love-hate situations. The band couldn't be better."

Lucinda heard herself parroting Falmouth, and shut up. Turning her back on the dewy moonish lemur, she grabbed Denise's arm, tugged the smaller woman to her side, so they stood hip to hip. They stepped in tandem, feeling an alliance beyond the grasp of language. They were the girls in the nameless band, the rhythm section.

"Let's go back and see that mountain goat with his crazy red penis."

"Maybe he'll catch her and fuck her."

"He'll never catch her. She always stays on the other side of that little fake mountain. The zoo made a mistake, they brought the wrong goats, she doesn't like him. He's going slowly insane."

"Maybe, but maybe she'll let him catch her. I think it might be today. I want to see."

"I bet they all fuck at night," said Lucinda. "The whole zoo. All night every night, when we're not looking."

through her kitchen's rear window on Reservoir Street Lucinda could see, over the rooftop of a tire shop and against a background of shaggy palms, the high rotating sign of the Foot Clinic. It depicted a cartoon foot with features and tiny limbs:

one side a happy, cared-for foot, beaming and confident, white-gloved hands jubilantly upraised, the other side a moaning, broken-down foot, neglected and weary, grasping at crutches and with its big toe wreathed in bandages. Lucinda's view took in a three-quarters slice of the sign as it turned in its vigil over Sunset Boulevard: happy foot and sad foot suspended in dialogue forever. The two images presented not so much a one-or-the-other choice as an eternal marriage of opposites, the emblem of some ancient foot-based philosophical system. This was Lucinda's oracle: one glance to pick out the sad or happy foot, and a coin was flipped, to legislate any decision she'd delegated to the foot god.

Beside the candle on her table lay half a Cafe Tropical Cuban sandwich in a nest of foil, a torn scrap of canary paper with a phone number scribbled on it, a Polaroid snapshot of a supine yellowish kangaroo in a band of shaded concrete, and a cordless telephone.

When Lucinda had parted from Denise and returned to the gallery she'd found the hubbub dissipated, the journalists and Falmouth gone, the fort held down by the interns, the two girls settled into a rhythm, answering the steadily blinking phones and transcribing complaints. Lucinda rejoined them. After the evening surge had peaked one of the interns leaned in at Lucinda's cubicle and passed her the scrap of paper.

"He said you'd know who he was," the intern announced drily.

Now, fingertips nudging the dangerous scrap of paper, the boundary-smashing digits, Lucinda glanced up. The foot sign completed a turn, face wheeling into view: sad foot. Lucinda left her phone untouched.

Instead she took the Polaroid to her desk and located a ball-point pen, an envelope, and a stamp. Writing left-handed to disguise her script, she lettered I NEED YOU in capitals on the photograph's fat bottom margin, practically engraving the words in the glossy sandwich of paper. Then, still with her left hand, she wrote MATTHEW PLANGENT on the envelope, and below it, Matthew's address. Slid the Polaroid into the envelope. Touched her tongue to the flap's glue and sealed it. Stamped it and put it in her purse.

# three

the song, "Shaft of Light, Piece of String," sounded fantastic. They were playing it in a narrow hallway, but the crowd was happy. You couldn't keep from thinking the stage should have been put at one end or another instead of in the middle of the hallway so we wouldn't keep having to crane their necks to acknowledge the audience on the other side, but nobody minded. Lucinda said she heard a rat or a squirrel under the stage, it was distracting. "Shaft of Light, Piece of String" had seven choruses. Bedwin really was a genius. The band finally had a name, but nobody could remember whether it was Famous Vomit Ferry or Long-Term Pity Houseguest, and hadn't the word "houseguest" already been used somewhere? Denise sang something that sounded like a hymn, it was unexpected for the drummer to sing but we tried to act cool about it, they didn't want to offend her because it was religious. The stage was too tall. The chorus of the new song went "I'm a little doughnut" but Matthew kept saying "I want a little doughnut." It was too late to correct him. The audience really liked it anyway. Famous Pity Magnet was really popular and they sounded really good.

The band was dreaming.

W e're going to have a party," Jules Harvey explained in his dry, blank voice, as he fingered his heavy black frames and gazed down at the tablecloth. Harvey sounded astonished by his own words, uncertain they'd reach his listeners' ears before wafting off in the breezeless air. Falmouth sat studying Lucinda for her response, his arms crossed against his suit as though bodily containing impatience. The three sat around a table on the Red Lion's patio, neglecting steins of afternoon lager that had been plunked down by a waitress in lederhosen. A rap beat blared from a car on the street below, fracturing the boulevard's gelled soundscape.

"Okay," said Lucinda, confused. Harvey, in his Detroit Tigers baseball cap and sneakers, and Falmouth, overdressed at one o'clock in a seersucker suit and yellow tie, had swept in together and nabbed her from her cubicle for the meeting. The two had bored her with small talk before finally announcing their project. Now she waited to understand.

"Jules is a promoter," said Falmouth. "We're collaborating on a happening."

"I have a rather large loft," said Jules Harvey apologetically.

"It's going to be a dance party," said Falmouth. "Only the rule is you can't bring anyone you know. And you have to wear headphones. You have to listen to whatever you prefer to dance to, your own mix. If people don't have their own headphones we'll provide them at the door, like neckties and jackets at a club. What I want is a sea of dancing bodies, each to their own private music. I might call it Party of Strangers. Or maybe Aparty, like *apart, y.*"

"I get it."

Falmouth held up a cautioning finger. "There's more. Instead of beginning and ending gradually and spontaneously, like the usual party, I want the start to be perfectly regimented. Everyone has to arrive at exactly such and such o'clock and begin dancing immediately. Latecomers will be turned away. And then at the end, same thing. I may buy a starter's pistol."

"Falmouth had been thinking the backdrop ought to be perfect silence," said Jules Harvey. "But I suggested it might be even better to have a band playing, very quietly, with nobody paying any attention."

"I thought your little consortium might want the gig," said Falmouth. He spoke grudgingly, as though Jules Harvey had persuaded him against his instincts. Harvey had a talent for insinuating himself, Lucinda suspected. She felt a pang of sympathy for Falmouth, usually so eager to patronize others, here so effortlessly co-opted.

"Attractive people playing and singing in the classic format: guitar, drums, singer, etcetera," said Jules Harvey. "Falmouth gave me the impression that you and your friends could answer the call. Only you must be able to play exceedingly quietly. Really, you should be nearly inaudible." He spoke with the same plodding earnestness with which he'd praised her armpit.

"I suppose it's possible," said Lucinda. She took a long drink of her beer.

"Between Jules's efforts and my own, we ought to stir up a certain amount of attention," said Falmouth. "Who knows? It could be the break you've been waiting for."

"I'll have to talk to the others," she said.

"Falmouth forgot to tell me the name of your band," said Harvey.

"We haven't—"

"Maybe there should also be food no one is allowed to eat," said Falmouth, his attention meandering. In his typical way, Falmouth now took it for granted that the band was enlisted. "Cooks might be preparing something to one side. Delicious smells emanating through the party. And then servers in black tie could load up trays and stand ready at the edges of the dance. Suddenly, just as they take a first step into the room, I fire the pistol a second time, the party's over, and everyone is whisked out of the room before they can eat anything."

She envisioned presenting this chance to the band: their first gig, a thing they'd have expected to come by way of Denise, their beacon of professionalism, or Bedwin or Matthew, who knew musicians—anyone but Lucinda, their self-taught bassist. Matthew, distrusting Falmouth, would take the offer for an insult. She'd need to emphasize Jules Harvey, the famous party promoter, and his rather large loft. They'd be forced to play inaudibly, sure, but to a huge crowd. Most bands debuted to barely anyone at all, to a handful of drunks. Here, they'd be an element in an artwork. Falmouth's allure, his knack for offhand success, would infect them. And Jules Harvey's eerie sincerity would ensure nobody mistook the band for merely one of Falmouth's mean jokes. Harvey would make it clear they were picked for a reason, attractive people in the classic format. After showing how quietly they could play they'd give evidence of what else they were capable of, the quiet, nearly overlooked band, the art band, the band not like any other.

She was the most beautiful woman I ever slept with. Except in a way I never did. It's a funny story, actually."

"Tell me." The other cubicles were dark. Falmouth had left early, his interest in complaint already wandering, perhaps overtaken by his Aparty. Lucinda was alone in the gallery when he called, her fabulous complainer. She'd switched off the lamp at her own desk and leaned into the shadow, beyond the spill of ambient light from the storefront's fluorescents. No one passing on the street would know she was there. No one expected her anywhere. There was no rehearsal. If he hadn't called her at the gallery she might have dialed his number, which nested in her pocket, inscribed on paper softened to tissue from handling. She might have dialed it or not. She might have again consulted the foot to decide. It didn't matter. He'd called.

"She was the kind of beautiful woman who makes other women angry," he said. "They'd see her and begin accidentally breaking stuff or getting stomachaches and needing to go home. She was a kind of beautiful catastrophe in that way. She'd ruin parties."

"I'm not like that," said Lucinda.

"Beautiful, or envious?"

"Envious."

"I had that feeling about you."

This was what she wanted to hear, his feelings about her. Yet he didn't know her. Lucinda and the complainer were occult to each other, their mingled voices a conspiracy of imagination. For all she knew he could be only blocks away. Yet for now, his previous existence on earth was fascinating and horrible and she had to know more.

"What made her so beautiful?" It sickened her slightly to ask, as though she were one of the women with stomachaches, fleeing parties.

"She was tall and smooth and strange," he said. "Like an alien, with impossibly long limbs. You couldn't keep from staring at her, picturing her in certain situations, all tangled in sheets."

"How did you meet?"

"She was the wife of someone I used to know. They got married when she was eighteen or nineteen, I think. He used to stand around guarding her all the time, as if he was shielding her body from a blast. She'd have this look on her face that was sort of bored and panicked at the same time. It was like she was a hostage and they were trying to find a place in the world to hide her. I pitied them in a lot of ways."

"What happened?"

"It was a few years later when I saw her again. At a dinner party. Their marriage had fallen apart, I never knew the details, but she was alone. I think by then she was trying to make up for some of what she'd missed, marrying so young. But it was hard for her. She stood out, she was too immaculate in a way, she had some kind of gawky elegance that made it difficult for her to get properly defiled."

"Go on."

"We talked. You know, about sex."

"And—"

"I told her I couldn't explain why but that I only wanted one thing from her, and that was to make her come with my mouth while she was watching television. And ideally while she smoked a cigarette, too, but she wasn't a smoker."

"You can't have everything."

"No."

"So that's why you never slept with her? Because the television was on?"

"It was just something to talk about the first few times. I'd talk and she'd listen, and laugh at me. She had this deep laugh, you didn't know where it came from because she had a normal, mild voice, but then this stomach-based laugh would chuckle out of her, like she was laughing at you with her whole soul. The laugh was revealing, but what it revealed was her distance. It let you know how far away she'd gone to hide from her body and from the world and the responses of all the men she'd met."

Lucinda didn't want to joke now, didn't want to risk interrupting his story. She waited, the only sound the humming of Falmouth's ionizer as it labored at the room's dead air. She could hear him listening, too, sensed his satisfaction at this deepening between them, her breath-held anticipation of his words.

"One night I guess she got tired of laughing and saying no and she took me to her apartment, this huge place she'd lived in during her marriage. Once she'd decided, we didn't discuss anything. It was a somber ritual, as if we felt answerable to some third party we didn't want to disappoint. She had a television but no cable, so we put in a video. Her former husband was a film scholar, he'd left all these videos behind. It was in another language, something Scandinavian. The glow was the only light in the room. I guess she was reading the subtitles. I couldn't."

Lucinda released a soft click from the well of her throat.

"It took a really long time. I think she must have watched half that movie. And when it was over she was still quiet. I could tell she was just waiting for me to leave. I assumed that was the end of it, but she called me about a week later and told me I could visit again if I wanted. This time it didn't take so long and when she came she started laughing at me, that same fathomless lunatic belly laugh. I was just kneeling there in my clothes between her long legs and I guess I looked sort of stupid. She sashed up her robe and just started laughing."

"I'd laugh too," said Lucinda softly.

"Of course you would."

"Finish the story."

"It became a regular thing for a while. I'd visit her apartment and she'd put in a video and sprawl on her chair in front of the television, it was a ratty yellow armchair, and throw her robe open. And she'd laugh afterward. She'd just look at me and laugh madly, and I'd laugh too. It was like I was escorting her on some long passage from where her reserve and her beauty had exiled her, only the voyage could never be finished for her. She'd come and laugh and then it would be time for me to go. Nothing was ever discussed. After a few times I began to push a little. I told her I wanted to tie her up, tie her to the bed or a chair, take away her control. I promised I wouldn't do anything she didn't want me to do, wouldn't do more than I'd done, if that was what she wanted. I only wanted to bind up her limbs and stop her from laughing, maybe, restore the trepidation she'd felt that first time. When I brought it up she'd only laugh and turn on the television. Then we'd drown ourselves in dialogue from foreign films and the little sounds she'd make and the flickers on the wall and the colors projected on her stomach and her filthy yellow chair. She always tried not to make any sounds until she had to. Then she'd explode and start laughing and send me out to my car. It was a perfect relationship, so I had to wreck it."

"How?"

"I kept pushing, trying to get her to allow me to tie her up. And one day she let me. I had no idea what to do, I'd spent all my energy just persuading her, never imagining it would come true. So, I brought over all my neckties and cinched her to the bed. I covered her eyes, too. And turned on the overhead light, which I'd never done. And then it was suddenly over. I had her there, I was able to stare as long as I liked. I could see her breathe and wait, her stomach trembling. But there wasn't anything left to do. I didn't say anything. I just went into the kitchen and ate some of her food. She began mewing, this sound that was practically like a kitten or a bat—meanwhile I was raiding the fridge. Then I found a pair of scissors, and I went in and silently cut the tie that held her right wrist to the bedpost, then placed the scissors on the table beside her, where she'd be able to find them. Then I left."

"That's it?"

"We never spoke again."

In the silence Lucinda studied the electronic surf of tone on the line, a sound like distant galaxies collapsing. Falmouth's gallery might have been a kind of capsule whirling in vast blank space. Then human sounds trickled in from the street—a slammed car door, a bubble of argument—and repainted the world.

"For a while I was thinking that was kind of a sexy story but it gets really depressing at the end."

"I should have warned you."

"When you left her there, was that your way of taking revenge? Because she didn't care about pleasing you?"

"I never thought of it that way."

"You never wished she'd touched you?"

"I suggested the arrangement in the first place."

"I still think it might have been revenge."

"It might be true."

"You don't know?"

"It's a secret, I guess."

"So you do know."

"No. I meant the other kind of secret. It's possible there's a reason I left her lying there, but I don't know it. Even before I left the room, all I could think about was what she might have to eat in the refrigerator. I could make up a reason but then I'd be lying to you. If it exists it's a secret from myself."

"She'd say it was revenge."

"I'm open to the suggestion. All I remember is her gawky limbs and that crazy laugh, the flicker of Swedish films across the arms of that filthy yellow chair, the color and texture of her pubic hair when I finally got to examine it in bright light. It's not some fable about revenge."

"I guess the best secrets from yourself are the ones that even if someone else tells them to you, you still don't know them."

"Sure."

"I can't decide if your story is funny or depressing."

"Maybe it's both. Haven't you ever noticed that whenever anybody wants to convince you that you ought to be interested in anything really gloomy, the first thing they tell you is how it's actually quite funny?"

"What about the girl in your story? Did she find it depressing, or funny?"

"I don't think it counted for that much one way or the other. We were only one another's astronaut food."

"What's astronaut food?"

"You know, stuff in little packets that you keep lying on the shelf. Everyone has some lying around. The people you imagine you might be with but you know you never really will be. The people who if you're in a couple but you're a little bored or restless you meet them for coffee a lot and the other half of your couple isn't really thrilled about it. Or if you're single, they're the people you're keeping on a mental list just so you don't feel like there aren't any possibilities. Friends who are almost more than friends but really, they're just friends. Astronaut food, bomb-shelter provisions. If you were ever going to have anything with them it would have happened already. Sometimes you even fall into bed with them, but it doesn't count for much. It's always a mistake to try to get any nourishment out of that stuff. But not a big mistake. That's the beautiful part, how the stakes are so low."

"Only if everyone agrees that they're mutual astronaut food."

"Oh, absolutely. You can screw up your astronaut food a million ways. Even just letting them know. Though they sense it at a certain level, nobody wants to be told. The worst is when someone falls in love and then gets all self-righteous about breaking up with their astronaut food, as if there's anything to break up about."

"What about the situation when someone is acting like they're only astronaut food, but really has hopes of something more."

"Yes."

"Would you say I'm astronaut food for you?" The question tumbled from her lips. He'd never asked her whether there was anyone in her life, never asked her age or name or what she looked like. But then what had she learned about him?

"I don't know," he said tenderly. "It's possible. Am I astronaut food for you?"

"I almost called you from my apartment last night," she said, hearing her breath interfere with the syllables, knowing he heard it too.

"Why didn't you?"

"The foot said no."

He hesitated. "Is the foot a friend of yours?"

"Yes."

"Well, then you should listen to him."

"The foot's not a he."

"Oh."

"I have to go now," she said, suddenly abashed.

"Why?"

"I haven't eaten dinner."

"Are you going to masturbate?"

"Not on the telephone."

bedwin opened his door with a shocked look on his face. Lucinda stood with a white, grease-spotty bag containing two piping slices fetched from Hard Times, the pizzeria at the base of the hill above which Bedwin's tiny cottage apartment was perched, hoping to bribe her way into his digs. The nature of his home life had been a subject of keen speculation among the other members of the band.

"Want something to eat?"

Bedwin only stared. He was fully dressed in his usual costume: sneakers, plaid shirt buttoned to his Adam's apple, analog wristwatch, glasses. Lucinda imagined him sleeping in it.

"Can I come in?"

"Oh, sure."

"Did I interrupt something?"

"No, I was just, uh, watching a movie."

"What movie?" She followed him through his door, into a low passage lined with book-tumbled shelves, claustrophobically close.

"It's called *Human Desire*. By Fritz Lang."

Bedwin lifted the takeout bag from Lucinda's hands and scuttled into the kitchen, stranding her in a room whose every surface was crazed with media. Records and videotapes and compact discs strained every shelf to its limit, along walls layered with ephemera: concert tickets, 45s thumbtacked through their spindle holes, and Magic Markered set lists retrieved from the floors of concert stages, many with chunks of duct tape still clinging to their edges. His two armchairs were populated by tottering books, piled so high they served as dusty dummy companions. The television, stacked with the videocassette player on a milk crate, faced an empty patch of carpet. Its screen displayed the black-and-white image of a locomotive, trembling in frozen static beneath the word PAUSE in blue.

Bedwin returned from the kitchen with two small plates in hand, the triangles of pizza draped over their edges. "I don't have any beer or anything."

"That's okay." She'd quaffed a beer beforehand, looking to take the edge off her panicky enthusiasm. "The movie good?"

He looked shocked again. "It's one of the ten greatest films of all time."

"So you've seen it before."

"I guess you could say I'm studying it."

"I don't want to interrupt if you need to—"

"No, it's fine. But if you want to watch it I don't mind rewinding to the beginning."

"That's okay."

"Sure," he said, his tone only slightly injured.

"I'd love to see it another time," she said. "I wanted . . ."

Bedwin waited, his pupils wide. The two of them stood balancing pizza on tiny plates, crowded together in the room's clear spot.

"Is there a place to sit in the kitchen?"

"Sure, sure."

They perched at two corners of Bedwin's red linoleum table, their pizza before them. Bedwin nibbled, ready to understand her invasion here. Lucinda imagined she could say or do anything and rely on his obedience, a disturbing prospect, actually. Perhaps she'd underestimated the responsibilities entailed in invading the sanctum of a mind as tender as Bedwin's. In the room behind them the player reached some limit and clicked off the film, the space filling with blue light and a dim undertone of static.

Her own agenda boiling within her, Lucinda tried to pacify herself with a few bites of pizza before pulling the crumpled yellow sheets from her bag and smoothing them across the table between them.

"Look, here's the thing," she said. "I have some more ideas for songs. Do you like 'Monster Eyes'?"

"It's so great," he said, with fannish sincerity and awe.

"Maybe we can do it again. Look."

The five sheets were headed with titles. Beneath them, fragments of lyrics lurched in urgent scrawl to the margins, oblivious to printed lines. The jottings resembled crazed dictation, perhaps some Ouija boardist's blind record. She hadn't examined them since fleeing the gallery, but she didn't have to. Bedwin would see and understand. Each notion would make the root of a song as good, as unexpected and pure, as "Monster Eyes." Bedwin only had to set them to music.

"What's that—'Astronaut Food'?"

"Yes."

"I like that." Bedwin murmured phrases to himself, discovering them aloud. "Secrets from yourself . . . bomb-shelter provisions . . ."

"And this one," she said, overeager, rustling pages. Bedwin flinched, taken aback. " 'Dirty Yellow Chair.' See?"

"Yes . . . it all looks terrific, Lucinda." He spoke gently, wonderingly.

"Nobody has to know I gave you these. Let's just pretend you came up with them yourself, okay?"

"You don't want to write them with me?"

"No. Just take them. You don't need any help from me, you know it."

"I shouldn't tell the others?"

"It'll confuse them. Matthew won't like it. You're our song-writer. These are just ideas, anyway. They'll be your songs."

"Sure, sure. Lucinda?"

"Yes?"

"Are you okay? Because you seem a little excited, I mean maybe a little bit upset about something."

"Nothing, I mean, nothing's wrong, everything's great."

"Okay, no problem, I was just checking."

"Maybe I'll let you get back to your movie now."

"You could watch a little. It's really a tremendously interest-ing film. Or at least finish your pizza."

"I'm not really hungry," said Lucinda. She stood, brushing her lips free of possibly imaginary flour. She'd barely eaten. She re-called the last words of her talk with the complainer and felt the urgent call of her fingertips to her own body. She ought to be in the bathtub, afloat in silence and dark, so that she could recap-ture the twilight realm of the phone call. She might even call him: she thought this for the pleasure of thinking it, even as she was certain she wouldn't. But she needed to be home, to dwell on their talk. Her errand had been essential: she needed to deliver the yellow crib sheets, the guilty jottings. Those were for the band, and they belonged here with Bedwin. She'd had to deliver them, and now she had to go. Even as she skirted the table's edge and high-stepped through the blue-glowing piles of books and records she realized she'd forgotten to tell Bedwin about the Aparty, the gig of playing silently. It didn't matter. The songs were more important. She'd brought them to him and he'd under-stood. She'd announce the gig to the band at their next practice.

Bedwin followed her halfway, magnetized in confusion, holding his slice up near his mouth.

"Thanks, Lucinda, for, you know, coming by."

"Sure. Forget it. Just write those songs."

"Yes."

"Goodbye, Bedwin."

Lucinda lowered a cauliflower head into her basket, where, with a five-pound bag of Integral Fare's own granola, it dragged at her arm like a cannonball. She hoisted the freight to her hip and browsed in the greens for something featherweight, a bundle of rocket or watercress to camouflage her sorry load. Integral Fare ought to issue backpacks for those like her, shoppers embarrassed to push a monumental rolling cart with items scant enough for the express line. As she reached into the display a robot sprinkler began its misting cycle, instantly soaking her sleeve.

In the early-evening presence of so many moodily lit vegetable shapes it wasn't remarkable to notice a slight pheromonal hubbub as shoppers ogled one another, or postured over their selections, waiting to be noticed. Tonight Lucinda felt a personal flutter, a disturbance in her field. A young redhead in a leather coat lingered pensively near a man in torn jeans. Her pursuit brought her edging through Lucinda's orbit. The man loaded a rolling cart with heads of cabbage and lettuce and bundles of beets and celery, a flaunt of healthfulness, Lucinda thought with irritation, even as she realized the man in jeans was Matthew.

He appeared oblivious to both women. His cast was grim, lip

bitten in ponderous consideration of kale and bok choy. Lucinda poked him in the waist with a carrot.

"Ow."

"Ever feel you're being watched?" she asked. Behind them the red-haired girl's posture tightened in disappointment. She melted off to another aisle.

"I didn't see you there."

"I didn't mean me. Several eyeballs were stuck to your pants. You ever notice that this produce section is a real meat market? Ha ha."

"Sorry?"

"When I haven't seen you for a while I forget how handsome you are," she said. "Like a model on a billboard advertisement for vegetarian cigarettes."

He blinked at her and fumbled at the cabbages in his cart. The robot sprayer arm finished its cycle. Lucinda heard the trickling of new moisture in the leaves. A scent of dampened mulch rose through the conditioned air.

"You're not too much fun. At least say something, like 'All cigarettes are vegetarian.'"

Matthew only stared. Lucinda felt the dawning of a new and original awkwardness between them. She'd relied on the band to enmesh them in something still near enough to a liaison, the tension of a bass player half turned to a singer, plumbing notes, jerking the song from his body. The voltage of the band's aspirations, fierce as lust. Here they were nothing but two shoppers, bearing bald homely groceries in opposite directions.

"It's good to see you," Matthew said. He patted her clumsily on the elbow, then withdrew.

Now she spotted the glitch of panic in his raccooned eyes, his extra day's stubble. "What's the matter?"

"Nothing."

"That's a really gargantuan salad you're making," she said.

"It's a lot," he confessed blankly.

She counted the green and purple heads in his cart, calculating volumes of leafy material. "Some sort of coleslaw sauna treatment, or are you throwing a dinner party?"

"I have a visitor."

"Someone I know?"

He regarded her evenly, with a still, small defiance.

"A sick friend?" she asked.

"I guess you could say that. Someone who needs my help."

Lucinda was silenced now.

"I think I should be getting back," said Matthew. He pivoted his cart toward the registers.

"I'll see you at rehearsals," she called to his departing back. She felt like the redhead now, a thirsting stranger. "Don't forget."

At home Lucinda boiled the cauliflower whole, suffused it with butter and pepper, then devoured it with knife and fork as if it were a soufflé. The dish was either lame and lonely, or grand, she couldn't decide, but consoled herself imagining translated French names—"white brain," possibly, or "virgin moon." She poured a scotch, just a small one, sat breathing its mellow fumes, barely drinking. Then wrecked the evening irretrievably by glancing in the hallway mirror for the foot's command: it smiled encouragement and she dialed the complainer's number. No answer. He had no machine. Each echoing chime of the unanswered line cast another band of shadow across her heart's floor. After twelve rings she gulped the scotch and re-treated to bed.

**t**he set list grew. Bedwin had written four new songs: "Dirty Yellow Chair," "Nostalgia Vu," "Astronaut Food," and "Secret from Yourself." He presented them to the band at the same afternoon rehearsal where Lucinda unveiled the news of the Aparty gig, the chance to play quietly in front of several hundred of Falmouth's well-dressed art friends. It was easy to picture them as tastemakers, rumormongers, a milieu capable of making a new band its pet overnight. Together, songs and gig, it presented an orgy of possibilities. Nobody knew what to say. The songs were so fine that Bedwin himself seemed astonished. The band's only outlet for its bewildered gratitude was to commence rehearsing diligently. So they shirked paying jobs and sleep, gathering four of the next five nights to burnish the treasury of new material. Talk grew respectfully minimal. Denise regularly fixed sandwiches for Bedwin at the breaks, assuming this care-taking duty without resentment. Matthew arrived on time and expressed no exasperation at the intervals of tuning among the instrumentalists, gazing fixedly at middle distances while waiting for the players to resume behind him, then carving deep into the material, despite seeming otherwise somewhat wasted, skinnier than ever. At each set's conclusion distraction overtook him, and he left before the others.

Lucinda held her secrets close. She felt a proprietary elation at having brought the others to this place. Yet hid inside the music, fingers throbbing on the neck of her instrument with a grace beyond her knowledge, agent of some higher purpose. The songs told her how to feel. She'd waited a week for a phone call which refused to come, then succumbed two nights in a row to the temptation to dial the complainer's number. For reward, only listened to his line howl in vacancy. She felt no impatience. Her complainer would reemerge and find her, the songs said so. In the meantime she dwelled in his words, now made plastic and catchy by Bedwin and the band. Bedwin had written a backup harmony vocal for "Astronaut Food." Since they only owned two microphones, Lucinda curled down to meet Denise at the mike stand mounted close on her snare drum to sing, "Am I just astronaut food for you? Are you gonna take me along to the moon?" The sentiment might have seemed plaintive or piteous, but she and Denise always felt beaming joy as their voices braided.

The fifth night in their siege of rehearsal, the last night before the Aparty, Bedwin said, with an air of pre-defeat: "What about 'Robot Head in Mourning'?" Everyone understood: the phrase was a possible band name. The band still didn't have a name and they'd grown embarrassed even to try. Proposals weren't so much shot down as left to perish in the air. They'd even resorted once to sticking pins in a dictionary, with no success.

"Sounds more like an album title than a band name," said Denise.

"Mourning like dead or morning like morning has broken?" asked Lucinda.

"I was thinking like dead but it doesn't matter," said Bedwin. "We could spell it different ways at different times."

"I saw a bumper sticker the other day that said POUR LOVE ON THE BROKEN PLACES," said Denise.

"I've been seeing that thing everywhere!" said Lucinda. "I saw it on a T-shirt the other day. What does it mean?"

"We could call ourselves 'The Broken Places.'"

"Don't you think that's pathetic?" said Matthew.

"Pathetic is good," said Bedwin. "Maybe we should use the word 'pathetic' in the name."

"The Pathetic Fallacies," suggested Lucinda.

"The Pathetic Chickens," said Bedwin.

"Why chickens?" said Denise.

"Okay, hens," said Bedwin. "The Pathetic Hens."

"That's terrible," said Denise.

"Okay, the Fallacy Hens," said Bedwin.

"We really need a name before the gig," said Lucinda.

Matthew was nearly out the door, his mike cord bundled and shoved underneath Denise's couch, his guitar case in hand.

"What about that one from before?" said Denise, looking up from cinching the screw on her hi-hat. "The opposite of a molar or something?"

"Not a molar," said Bedwin. "The opposite of a wisdom tooth. Idiot Tooth."

"Yeah, Idiot Tooth, I like that one, I always think about it."

"How much can you like it if you can't even remember it?" said Lucinda. She tucked her bass into the felt bed of its case. "Anyway, wasn't there a band called Mystery Tooth?"

"Spooky," said Bedwin, almost under his breath.

"What?"

"Spooky, Spooky Tooth."

"Why does there always have to be something self-deprecating in the name?" said Matthew from the kitchen doorway. His beard was a week old now, a black frost that had overtaken his sallow cheeks nearly to his eyes. "What was that other name you guys liked? The Tedious Knives?"

"Knifes," said Bedwin.

"What?"

"It was knifes, with an 'f.'"

"Tedious, forlorn, morbid, crappy, futile."

"The Futiles?" suggested Denise.

"Let Falmouth decide," said Matthew. "I'm sure he'll have a suggestion. Maybe he should bill us as the Papier-mâché Band. Or the Deaf-mutes." He departed, not quite slamming Denise's door. The rest were silent and unnerved in his aftermath, their songs all chased away. Bedwin slowly wound his cord around his amp's handle, blinking at the floor. Denise leaned into her fridge and took out a beer. She waved the bottle at Bedwin, who shook his head. Lucinda stuck out her hand and Denise passed her a cold bottle.

"Things feel a little weird," Bedwin ventured.

"It's the gig," said Denise. "We're all a little cuckoo."

"We sound good."

"We sound great."

"The new songs are okay, huh?" Bedwin didn't meet Lucinda's sudden glance.

"They're the best songs," said Denise. She put down her beer and opened her arms to Bedwin. He tolerated her embrace, his shoulders square, terror swimming in his eyes.

"I guess I'll go home now," said Bedwin.

After he'd shambled through the door Denise said, "So, what's the matter with Matthew?"

"That's not my department anymore."

"Sure, but what's your theory?"

Lucinda gobbled her beer and swallowed hard before speaking. "My theory is he has a new girlfriend who doesn't speak such good English."

"I'm not sure I understand you."

"Maybe hostage is a better word."

"Does this have something to do with the zoo?"

Lucinda nodded, wide-eyed.

"You want something harder than that beer?"

<br>

**t**he two figures tumbled up the stairway in sloppy tandem, index fingers pressed to their whiskey-swollen lips, elbows at each other's ribs. They left the hallway's lightbulb chain unpulled, as if illumination was their enemy, and so tripped on the stairs and over their feet. The banisters and stairs, even the walls of the stairwell felt muffled in dust, but beneath the dust's mousy odor the drunken sleuths might have detected another scent, an acrid clue to what they were after, urine from another sphere. It was strong enough to bite its way even through their occluded noses. They sniffed their own fingertips stupidly, shrugged in the dark, advanced on creaking tiptoe.

"You got the key?"

"Fssshh."

Inside the apartment, Denise flattened like a moth against the white hallway, pinned in moonlight that spilled through the kitchen. Lucinda slid past her, teeth bared and eyeballs bugged in commitment to their idiot foray. Their noses said they neared some goal. The rooms throbbed with mulchy life force, festering salad, mammalian sweat.

Matthew slept with his door open, sprawled on his back, nude outlines covered by a thin sheet. His penis was stiff under the sheet, a totem draped in pale shadow, nighttime body divorced from mind, rehearsing its secret forces. The invaders froze, shared a glance of dread, gnawed the insides of their cheeks. Matthew's tongue lolled from his mouth, his head strained into its pillow as though smashing through dreams. Denise and Lucinda edged crabwise through the spotlight of the doorway, hands flat to the wall.

Past him, the smell was stronger. The room they discovered, Matthew's parlor, with television, stereo, couch, held no answers. Lucinda duckwalked into its middle to examine its corners. There was no animal besides themselves.

At first sight the bathroom appeared empty. Yet here, their noses testified, was the source. Their eyes adjusted to the dimness as they bumped into the middle of a checkerboard tile floor strewn with celery butts and shards of cabbage. The invaders peered together into the only secret place remaining, a clawfoot bathtub glowing like an ivory icon in the gloom.

Shelf the Flyer gazed up at them, her yellow eyes training calmly on each of theirs in turn. The kangaroo lay on her side, filling the waterless basin of the tub, elegant legs spread like a book, neck and forepaws and tail slack as a sleeper's. A trail of kangaroo piss beaded to the tub's drain.

Denise mimed a scream. Lucinda clutched her around the shoulders. Knees tangling, heels skating in lettuce slime, they nearly tumbled to the floor. Shelf only blinked and tightened her whiskers, didn't shift another muscle.

Lucinda held up a finger in a plea for stillness from Denise, then lowered Matthew's toilet seat, slid jeans and underwear to her thighs, plopped down and peed, inspired to seek relief herself. She left it unflushed. Let it be their calling card, a reply to the stink. Matthew would likely credit it as some prodigious act of the kangaroo's.

As Lucinda and Denise turned from the dim bathroom to the moonlit corridor the figure lurched into view—or had he stood there longer, just listening? Matthew loomed and swayed, wreathed in his sheet, eyes turtled in bafflement.

"Lucinda?" he croaked.

Caught, the drunken women only stared.

"This is so totally fucked up."

Now they ran for the doorway, still mute, as if by fleeing they might persuade Matthew to retreat to dream and incorporate them as apparitions. Forget any clues they left, the front door they now unlocked or their handprints smearing in the stairwell's dust. The essential thing was to give no testimony. The kangaroo in the bathtub had understood this principle, and kept cool. It was already impossible to be certain they'd seen her.

Lucinda slid through more dark, past Falmouth Strand's desk, on tiptoe again though there was no one to fool. It was two, three, or four in the morning, she couldn't tell, wore no watch. Lucinda wasn't ready to face her empty bed or the mocking twin faces of the foot sign. She'd delivered Denise to her own door, piloting her car on the empty Sunset Boulevard soberly, gingerly. Now, here alone in the gallery, she still felt drunk.

Seated at her unlit cubicle she lifted the phone and dialed the first six digits of the number she'd memorized without intending to, then circled her finger over the last, daring fate or at least gravity to cause it to descend. At that moment she heard herself snort or snore loudly, then woke with a jerk from some sudden depth, her head elbow-propped on the phone's receiver, its mouthpiece mashed to her lips and slathered in saliva. The line rang.

"Hello," he answered on the third ring.

"I called you," Lucinda said stupidly.

"Yes."

"I'm sorry," she said. "Were you asleep?"

"Nope."

"Mishomnia?"

"I was just awake."

She widened her jaw, licked her lips, tried to gather herself. "Why didn't you call me?"

"You were waiting?"

Lucinda moved the phone's receiver from her head in confusion, as if the complainer lived within the instrument. The object gripped in her hand told her nothing, might as well have been a hair dryer or thermos. For an instant she weighed replacing it in its cradle. Instead she returned it to her ear and discovered again his breath hushed against a backdrop of howling static and her own mental buzz.

"I want to see you," she said.

"I don't know if that's a good idea."

"I need to."

"I'm free tomorrow night."

Lucinda issued a sound like a thwarted sneeze.

"You know the Ambit Hotel?" he said. "Downtown, on Sixth."

"Uh, sure."

"Meet me at the rooftop bar at nine."

"Okay, wait, how will I know you?"

"We'll be the only two people looking for each other."

"Okay."

"Nine o'clock, don't forget."

"Okay."

"Get some sleep."

"Okay."

"And drink a large glass of water, you'll feel better."

Lucinda nodded and hung up the phone.

**t**he morning light, when Lucinda cinched open her crumb-gummed lids, was unwelcome. She raised her face from a sleeve smeared with sleep drool, then she turned and saw the polished tops of Falmouth's shoes. He touched her arm when she stirred.

"You poor pathetic wretch," he said caressingly.

"Oh, Falmouth."

"You're like a child marinating in your own crimes. You smell wrong."

Falmouth stood before her in his customary suit, a trim figure silhouetted in daylight, a Styrofoam coffee cup braced in his fingertips. One collar point was disarranged, straying upward from its home in his jacket, a poignant breach. His face betrayed tenderness.

"What time is it?" she said.

"Morning."

"All you do is work, Falmouth."

"Nothing matters but work. Someday you'll grow up and then you'll understand."

"My head hurts."

"It should hurt."

"We had band practice and then Denise and I drank whiskey."

"You're unsuited for this world. Your only recourse is to become a rock star. Anything else is beyond you."

"We're good, Falmouth."

"We'll see about that. Go home and put yourself to bed."

"Don't you need me today?"

"You're fired. My interns can answer the phones. They're better than you anyway."

As she roused herself from the cubicle Lucinda felt a sweet nostalgic stirring of affection, almost like green shoots of horniness under the pavement of her hangover. Perhaps the nearer you came to abandoning a romance, evaporating it in friendship, the more piercing and beautiful the trace that remained. Watching Falmouth turn to his lonely desk, place his cup so delicately on its coaster, scowl wholly to himself as he browsed voice mail on his speakerphone, it occurred to Lucinda that one day her well-dressed friend would die. Perhaps then she would stand by Falmouth's graveside and understand that he was the love of her life.

The sentiment, foolish or not, struck her as worthy of the complainer. At that instant Lucinda recollected the rendezvous, at the gaudy rooftop bar, only hours away, and her throat was scalded by a hiccup laced with the essence of vomit.

The Ambit's rooftop was like a three-dimensional magazine Lucinda browsed with her whole body. It made her feel irrelevant, unseen, blurred with age. She milled among pink and green cocktails held aloft by peach and mocha teenage limbs.

Each, cocktails and limbs, seemed lit by a similar incandescence. The starless night above her shuddered, too close. The complainer was nowhere, lurked behind no potted palm. No man examined her for any purpose whatsoever. No person was alone in that place besides Lucinda. She wandered for what felt to be years, then ordered a scotch, a double, slurped to the bottom, and headed for the elevator.

Another party had formed in the lobby. The valet had abandoned his post, draped his jacket over his abdicated parking stand. Instead he hunched over the handles of a nearby soccer table, madly spinning the posts studded with podlike replica players. He strained heedlessly at the dials, trying to alter the ball's trajectory with his knees and hips, emitting grunts and shrieks, shaking his head to free his bangs from his eyes. His opponent, a large man, stood calm and stolid with his back to Lucinda, weight equal on his eagled legs, merely twitching his wrists.

It was the valet who noticed her. He straightened to show his readiness, despite dereliction of post and uniform. The large man flipped the dial once more, unfairly plopping the ball into the valet's unguarded net, where it came to rest like a grape in a sock. Then turned. He was beautiful in a puffy, slightly decrepit way. His features, in the patio's reddish light, appeared like a painted cameo fringed by his white-streaked mane of hair. His nose and chin were each deep-dimpled, his eyelids baggy above and below, his face resembling in its totality the male organ itself. The man's clothes were loose, possibly camouflaging flab, his shirt's top buttons undone to show more white-infested hair rising to mask his clavicle, sleeves sloppily rolled to the elbows, corduroy pants belted uselessly low, not holding anything together. He was unmistakable. The person playing table soccer with the valet was the person she'd come here to discover.

"Complaints?" he said.

"One or two, I suppose."

"You probably think I'm late," he said. "Actually, I was on the roof at eight thirty. But I couldn't bear the noise, so I came downstairs."

"Why choose it in the first place?" she said, unable to disguise her peevishness. She handed the valet her ticket, wrapped in a pair of dollar bills. It shooed him, at least.

He shrugged. "This place is convenient to my house. And I figured it was a backdrop where you'd stand out."

Did he refer to her age? He didn't have any leg to stand on, himself. Beside him the valet was a child. She didn't mind his seniority, though. It suited her.

"You could have picked a place that was empty," she said petulantly.

"Would you have agreed to meet me in such an establishment?"

"I wouldn't have waited an hour, I'm sure of that. But now I see that wasn't necessary in the first place."

"Let me make it up to you."

"I just asked for my car."

"Perfect," he said. "I walked here."

"You live that close?"

He stepped across the patio that housed the table soccer, shrinking the distance between them. "You make that sound like an accusation," he said softly. "I hope we haven't gotten off on the wrong foot. I guess you're ticked you were waiting upstairs while I was down here the whole time. I'd chalk it up to my compulsive need to disappoint." He took her by the elbow, enfolding her in his billowy body, and opened the passenger door of her car, which now stood running in the driveway. Lucinda felt a giddy paroxysm of relief as her grievance dissolved. The complainer was recognizably himself. That was all she required.

The complainer ushered her into the seat, then stepped around the car and slid in at the wheel, groping for the lever to slide the seat back to make room for his legs and his fantastically large sneakers under her dashboard, loudly crumpling paper refuse behind the seat. He dismissed the valet, his former opponent, with a cheery wave. Then turned her car from the hotel's driveway onto Sixth Street, into downtown's empty canyons, his brow consternated as he peered past his knuckles, through the windshield. Hesitant to stare, Lucinda instead tasted with her whole body his significant displacement of the car's atmosphere, the rustle of his aura. He was clumsy and beautiful and absolutely real.

On a stepped pavilion a smudged man maneuvered a shopping cart to the lip of a vast inhuman fountain, alone amid sentinel buildings. He might have been the first mortal figure to cross that plain, a Thoreau approaching his Walden. In the passenger seat, waiting to know their destination, Lucinda felt encompassed by an oceanic tenderness that bloomed beyond the space of her car to cover the far solitary bum and his cart.

"Everybody's got wheels," she said.

"Sorry, I just left mine at home."

"That's not what I meant," she said, too dreamy to explain.

"I don't like to drive anyplace I can walk," he said, squinting at the street before them. "I know that outlook's a rarity in this burg. Still, you learn things at ground level. Don't get me wrong, though, I love my car. My car is my friend."

Lucinda labored to breathe, as though he'd robbed her car of its spare oxygen, inhaled it all himself. His shaggy gray hair and shoulders seemed to balloon toward her. Tiny rivulets flowed along her ribs and the backs of her knees. On the barren roadway, streetlamps illuminated the Datsun's interior in slow-flickering bands. Under cover of a flare of dark Lucinda placed herself against him, rubbed her chin on his arm through the thin, and slightly damp, cloth of his shirt.

"I'm not nervous, but then again I'm not not nervous," he said, without turning. "I find I actually don't want to disappoint you."

"You don't."

"Or be disappointed."

At the block's end, freeway on-ramp in sight, the complainer leaned her Datsun to the left, pointed it at the darkened curb at the foot of another tower, and rolled it to, then over, the curb. The car's nose bonked into a metal cable box on the sidewalk, producing a grinding noise. The complainer turned the key in the ignition, killing the engine. They perched there, tilted across the curb, facing the wounded cable box through the windshield.

"If your car's hurt I'll pay for any damages."

"I'm sure it's fine." Lucinda slanted her knees, drawing herself across the gearshift. The two of them lurched together, jaws fitting bonily in place, his imperfectly shaved upper lip chafing hers. He pawed the small of her back, fingers soft and huge like a pastry bear claw. She encouraged him, touched arms and shoulders through his flimsy shirt. The windows fogged, the Datsun's interior massing with exhaled steam. The car might explode, she thought, as she tugged free to consider him.

"What's your name?"

"Carlton. Carl."

"Lucinda."

"Lucinda the complaint girl."

"Carlton Complainer."

"Say Carl."

She said it into his mouth. His hands tangled in her clothes, his clubby fingertips working beneath her brassiere to bridge her ribs, as though measuring her breast. When she opened her eyes she found him inspecting her at close range. Her heart thudded against his palm.

"What?"

"You're beautiful."

"Thank you."

"I want to take your clothes off and do things to you."

"I want you to do things to me too."

"But not in the car."

"Okay."

"I'll have to drive us someplace."

"Your place is close."

"No."

She didn't understand, didn't care. "Should we go to my apartment?"

"Back to the hotel, I think." His questing hand toyed with the elastic threshold at her hip bone, made a sudden incursion below.

"Wait, uh, I can't think when you're doing that."

"I need neutral surroundings. This is confusing enough as it is."

"Oh," she sighed, pressing herself to his suddenly irresistible hand. She felt she could detect the exact texture of the whorls that tipped his wide fingers. The car teetered with her motion, as if on a crumbling cliff.

"Also they've got really good room-service burgers at that hotel."

"Okay."

The valet unblinkingly reclaimed her Datsun at the entrance, only panning his gaze to note the scuff the car's bumper had gained since he'd seen them last. Lucinda stood to one side at the check-in, swaying slightly, while the complainer registered. His touch had concentrated her blood somewhere between stomach and knees, leaving her higher brain entirely to the double scotch, which had perhaps been waiting in abeyance for this moment. The desk clerk, another child, handed over a single key card.

The room was full of unornamented blond wood in clean lines, gleaming chrome fixtures, low glowing lamps, and a vast stainless steel tub, big enough for two kangaroos. Lucinda unlaced her sneakers and sprawled on the king-size bed, framing herself in the sea of cushions, but the complainer turned from her, in no hurry now. Rapidly browsing the complimentary CDs, he clicked one into the player—jazz—then crouched at the minibar. He tossed several miniature bottles to clank against one another in an indented billow of the bed's comforter.

"Something brown," he said. "Rum and Coke?"

"What?"

"You taste brown."

"Scotch."

"Whiskey's what we've got."

"Fine. Just come over here soon already."

Without turning, he said, "Take off your clothes." He spoke wearily, as if imperfectly resigned to his role.

Lucinda almost hurt herself getting sweater, shirt, and unfastened brassiere over her head in one clump. The undergarment had been rotated beneath her armpits without her noticing, to form a kind of straitjacket. Tugging the ball of clothing from the neck, she poked herself in the eye. She slid her pants off too, catching her socks with her thumbs so they cocooned within her pants legs, another soft sculpture she deposited at bedside.

Only after she sat, trembling slightly, knees folded, feet crossed under her ass, did he turn and hand her a tumbler, then place himself on the bed's edge beside her. Some sadness in his eyes made her attempt a joke. "We used to have so much to say to each other."

"It's different now, yes," he said, apparently taking her at face value.

"Why?"

"We're creating secrets now, instead of telling them."

"Secrets from who?"

"Whom."

"From whom."

"That depends on who you tell your secrets to. Open your legs."

She did. A long moment passed before he spoke again. "Don't tell me you don't confide in anyone."

He placed his hand on her thigh. Her voice trembled lightly, low in her throat, as she said, "Not anyone. Not right now." The music in the room was distant, muffled by the pulse in her ears.

"The world is full of tellers. You can't even sit in a movie theater without hearing people share their thoughts."

"Not me," she managed.

"People are frightened of secrets, they remind them of death. Everyone tells just one person, but that person tells a thousand others."

"Not me."

"What about the complaint line?"

"I haven't told anyone about you."

"You will."

"Not if you don't want me to."

"You can tell anyone anything you want, my name, how we met, whatever. But let's create one real secret, let's lock something in this room forever. Like a rock sitting on a beach somewhere, through all time and space."

His fingers fanned across her stomach, again as if taking her measure. His thumb stretched beneath the curve of her, still not touching where he'd gone so suddenly before. She felt it was possible he could lift his hand and she'd find herself raised to the ceiling aloft.

"You can drink if you want," he said.

"Thank you."

"Do you want me to put my fingers inside you?"

"Please, yes."

"Two?" He raised his glass and uncurled paired fingers to show them to her.

"Yes."

"Only if you promise it's a secret forever. I don't care if it seems stupid to you, just a common act, no big deal. You can't ever describe this to anyone, neither can I. The way it feels, the look I see on your face, even just the fact that I'm going to do the particular thing I'm going to do."

"Please do it now."

"Promise."

"Why?"

"Because if it's a secret it's going to change how it feels. I want you to feel that." He sipped from his tumbler once more and set it aside.

"I promise."

One hand still bridged on her stomach, he reached with his other for her mouth. Lucinda gobbled his fingers avidly, slicking them. She heard her own zoological sounds, not only a snort as she widened her throat and breathed around his knuckles but also a hum and squeak deep in her chest.

"Don't give it a name," he said. "Don't even mention it to me."

"Uhnn."

"This doesn't need a name," he repeated, then moved his two fingers from her mouth and pushed them inside her.

"Oh, god." She took another drink, too much, and when she tried to swallow felt a sticky trickle of whiskey leak from the corners of her mouth, over her chin.

"Enough now," he said, and took the glass from her.

"Don't take your hand away," she said, her voice very small.

"Shhh. I won't."

"I'm—"

"Shhh." He moved deeper, pressing his thumbprint to her

clit. She abruptly came, shuddering against his whole arm with her swaying body, grasping at his back through his damp shirt.

the jazz ran out sometime without Lucinda noticing. He never restarted it, though they quit the bed several times to rearrange the lights, to draw the shades against the wall of offices that faced them, to run water in the basin to splash and slurp, to wash her scent off both their faces, though not before she'd sampled herself from his chin and nose. Lucinda was in a hotel robe and then out of it again. His body, once he removed his clothes, was thick. More generous than Matthew's, than anybody's. It surprised her how little she minded. His penis too. His hair, white at his throat, darkened below the curve of his stomach, as though night's setting had recorded itself across the field of his body. The television was on for a while, music videos they drowned with their own groans. When her foot swept a miniature bottle from blocking the digital clock face it read one thirty.

He forced her to wait once until she couldn't wait anymore and then when she came it was enormous, and she began laughing and couldn't stop for a while.

"That was the funny one," he said.

"Are you counting?" she said, still laughing.

"Sure, and giving them all names too, and that was the funny one."

"What were the others?" She panted to a halt.

"The fast one, the big one, the ugly one, and the one where you kicked me."

"The funny one was the big one."

"You can have your own names."

"You weren't there, you don't know." She laughed again. "And none of them were ugly. Fix me another drink."

"Another another."

"Yes."

Unexpectedly he was shy, donning his robe each time he went to the minibar.

"Carl?" It was the first time she'd said his name since the car.

"Yes?"

"Who is this a secret from?"

"Nobody, really. Not on my end."

"Oh."

"You?"

"I don't know. Maybe."

They were both in robes when the room-service guy, another eager child in a hotel costume, arrived with two flying saucer–shaped covers, lifting them like a magician to present their hamburgers. He placed the tray on the foot of the bed and while the complainer scribbled on the check he gawked at the state of the room with open delight. He thanked them and told them to have a good night like they were beautiful and crazy, then backed from the room in dazzled wonder, as if having gazed on the masters of some performance art. The complainer muted the television, the bejeweled rappers and squirming entourages now trapped behind aquarium glass. He slapped at tiny bottles of ketchup and mustard, pooling them, red and yellow side by side, in the center of his plate, then dipping his burger's bitten edge to swirl the colors together.

"I think the staff likes us," Lucinda said through a mouthful of hamburger. The warmth of the meal drew her toward helpless drowsiness.

"Probably they're massed in the hallway with their ears to the wall." He wore mustard on his upper lip. "Probably I could make a room-service call without the telephone."

"More whiskey."

"You haven't finished the last one."

"More burgers," she said, raising her burger.

"More bed, more music, more night."

"Room service, bring me a room."

"Exactly."

The liquor ran out and he kept making her drink water, insisting she'd thank him later. Maybe that was because he was older, maybe that was what passed for wisdom in a place and on a night like this, between two such people as themselves. Lucinda sucked droplets from the last of the little bottles instead, slurped the residue from her glass. Burger wreckage still at their feet, she said, "Let's make another secret." She curled in his lap and parted his robe and tried to raise him again, fruitlessly. He was spavined, mushy as a bar of soap.

"Here, drunk girl," he said, beckoning her up to the headboard. "You want to make a secret?"

"Yes."

"Lie back."

"Okay."

"Now pick up the telephone."

"Who am I calling?"

"Someone you shouldn't."

"Who's that?"

"I don't know, but you do. The maybe person, from before."

"The maybe person?"

"The one this is maybe secret from. Everyone has someone they shouldn't call."

She looked at him horrified, delighted.

He brushed his stubbly chin across her thighs, moved below. "Go ahead."

"It's too late," she said, not even glancing at the clock, which had whirled irretrievably past two, three.

"If there's one thing I know it's that it's never too late."

"I'll make noise."

"You'll control yourself."

"Okay, but wait, ah, just do that for a minute."

"Sure, but dial the phone."

Matthew's number rang three times, then clicked through to the false ring of voice mail. She knew it too well. "I'm getting his machine," she whispered.

"Leave a message," said the complainer, his mouth full, the words mashed into her.

"Saying what?" she panted.

"Sing something," he said. "Make up a song."

At the voice mail's tone she began. "Kangaroodle roo, pouchie the kangaroo, don't make kanga dootie on the floor ohhhh nooooh . . ." Gasping, she covered the receiver with her palm.

"Nice," he whispered. "Another verse." A waft of herself rose with his face from between her thighs, penetrated even her whiskey-dimmed nostrils.

"Kangaroodle dee, don't make any pee, don't make fun of me, you sad and glorious roo, you dootie pooper you . . ."

The complainer's mouth began to make her come again. She

wrestled the phone onto its cradle with spasming fingers, not before appending a pleasure-drenched chortle, a kind of hoot-gasp, to the message she'd left.

"Now you," she breathed.

"Now me what?"

"Now you on the phone. Now I do you."

"Drunk girl, I've got nothing left, haven't you noticed? Besides, I've got no one to call."

"I thought everyone did."

"Everyone except me."

"I'm not drunk."

"Your eyes are x's."

The sex ran out and now tangled in their robes and still atop the bedcovers and with the lights and television on they dozed, and then more than dozed, fell fast asleep, despite never having decided to, or not Lucinda, anyway. She passed out picturing herself dressing and retrieving her car, even as her beard-chafed cheeks and kiss-swollen lips moused in the nest of his elbow, one arm thrown across his stomach and one leg cantilevered over the tray which had been set just barely aside, so when she woke briefly, early light seeping in to delineate the curtain's edge, her foot dipped into ketchup and mustard and crumbs. She grunted, whisked the foot clean as she could with sleep-numbed fingers, then tucked it beneath her robe, shivering. The complainer snored beside her, and murmured too. Before she fell asleep again she thought she heard the words "more love on," or perhaps it was "pour love on." Or she might have imagined it entirely.

———

Lucinda woke in a cocoon of ripe headache, her senses withdrawn against the obnoxious fact of daylight, the planet's insufferable expedition through widths of light and dark. The man she'd slept beside had gone from the bed but she sensed him operating somewhere, manipulating gaily clanking artifacts outside her range of tolerable awareness. She touched her eyelids, tender wallets of pain, felt her orbs rustle within.

"Coffee?"

She made him out, a mass diffusing the glare.

"What time is it? Is it afternoon yet?"

"It's pushing afternoon."

"I have a gig tonight," she said. "My band, I mean."

"Here."

The coffee smelled like an enemy. "I think I need a drink, actually."

"I'd have to let them in to restock the minibar."

"I want a drink in my house. Drive me home."

"I'd have to drive your strange little car."

"What's strange about my car?"

"It bumps into things."

Lucinda pulled him, dressed, to her side of the bed. Hunching free of the binding sheets and robe, she squirmed bare limbs across him, and briefly humped his leg, a leftover animal temblor, then fell back. He was enormous, she saw now. Beneath his clothes he was a hill to climb, pink and hair all over, impossible to encompass. She wasn't through trying. Let the hellish sunshine make its case, the previous night wasn't finished. She and the complainer were a secret buried here, at the world's unreachable core, beyond the encroach of her headache or any other contradictory evidence. She needed to keep him near. Not in the hotel, though. She needed to take him to her apartment, show him the foot sign, her former god. She needed him to hear her play her bass, see her practice her art. And she needed to do something to him that would make him at least once more as gloriously deranged as he'd made her again and again in the hotel bed.

"Yes," she said.

"Yes what?"

"Drive me home in my strange little car."

The freeway was like a saddle on the splayed city, a means both of mastering it and of shrinking from intimate contact with its surfaces. The complainer handled her Datsun capably, zipping across lanes. Lucinda watched exits blink past, Glendale, Alvarado, Rampart. When the chance came for Silver Lake she bit her tongue.

"Here, take Western." She pointed him off the freeway, suddenly inspired. "Park on the right. This is my favorite liquor store. The Pink Elephant. It's beautiful. Look at that Dumbo mural, it's like cave art. This city is full of primitive geniuses. If they put that in a gallery it would sell for a million dollars. I don't know why they haven't been sued by Disney."

"Maybe they're owned by Disney."

"Get us a fifth of something. No more stupid little bottles."

"Blue label?"

"At this point I'd take yellow or even green label."

He returned, slid a bottle in a bag down by her feet, then resumed the wheel. She motioned for him to aim the Datsun down Hollywood Boulevard. She halted them in front of the

Celebrity Motor Inn, a three-story palace of neon and rotting palms, ironwork skyway suspended between its wings, a majestic relic amid the ruined commercial strip. Skyway lit from beneath, the inn was like a piece of day-for-night footage against the pale sky.

"Nothing against your Ambit room-service burgers but that's what I call a hotel."

"I thought we were going to your apartment."

"I changed my mind. I don't see your place, you don't see mine. Fair's fair."

"I'll go sign the register," he said, pulling into the parking lot. "Mr. and Mrs. Dead Noon."

a t the shop on Sunset the band's drummer frowned as she packed a shipment for delivery, a mammoth latex implement not modeled on any human part, shaped instead as a squirrel riding a dolphin, each peeping through a separate cellophane window of the product's glossy cardboard package. She bound it with its invoice in a triple thickness of bubble wrap, feeling irritated still to be at work. She'd swapped shifts with another clerk to earn her freedom this afternoon, and her substitute should have appeared by now. The drummer hoped to nap before the time came to load her kit into the trunk and backseat of her car. The party promoter had made the band promise to arrive for a sound check at five, though how it mattered wasn't clear, since they were meant to be inaudible. Putting the package aside, the drummer dialed the phone, not for the first time. There was no answer, and she didn't leave a message.

Above Hyperion Boulevard, the band's guitarist sat cross-legged on his carpet, bathed in blue light, his mouth open, as his videocassette recorder slow-motioned through a passage in *Human Desire*, a bar scene, Glenn Ford tussling with a drunken Broderick Crawford over Gloria Grahame. The guitarist seemed uninterested in the performances, instead drew nearer to the screen, trying to decipher the words written on signs pinned to the walls of the bar, which at the level of resolution of his television was impossible. The guitarist picked his nose with a curled forefinger and squinted closer. His other hand absentmindedly cradled his crotch. The blue figures on-screen swam forward, captives of slow motion.

On Effie Street the band's singer stood wielding a knife at his kitchen counter. He still wore his T-shirt and underwear, the costume he'd decided to wear to bed since an intrusion into his house the night before last. He'd slept late after lying awake until dawn, having been woken by his phone ringing at some odd hour. The singer chopped a bundle of unrinsed kale into a careless salad. The *Los Angeles Times* lay across his counter, a copy pilfered from the doormat of the singer's neighbor across the hall. He'd scoured the City section for an article which he'd hoped to see but which hadn't appeared. Its absence dismayed him. The remaining sections were unread. Though it wouldn't have been difficult for the singer to refold the paper and return it to the doormat, it was instead destined to be thrown over his bathroom tile, to absorb certain spillings and stainings. As he switched from the kale to a mass of celery, the singer mused on the voice-mail message he'd listened to at dawn, the baby-talk song with its strangely accurate, if mocking, encapsulation of his dilemma. The singer felt lonely. He decided to take his next chance to entrust the band's bass player with his secret. After all, she already knew it.

On Hollywood Boulevard, in pale afternoon light bent through tweed curtains, the band's bass player drew herself, panting, from the still-trembling body of her lover, who lay with his head tipped over the foot of the bed. His hands, which had encircled her, palms nudging her breasts, now fell to his own thighs. His blotched penis draped in an arc to his stomach. There were no robes here. No music. They'd poured from the new bottle into plastic cups, which sat in a spilled pool of whiskey on the side table, beside the telephone. The bottle was half empty, but the bass player didn't feel drunk anymore. She undoubled her knees and stretched her feet to cradle his ribs. Leaning back, her sweaty shoulders sealed like a decal to the headboard. The motor inn was a perfectly tawdry arena. If possible she'd have her car and apartment destroyed by remote control, and begin again from here. It was as if the hotel rooms they'd inhabited were the telephone line they'd dwelled in earlier, now expanded to contain the whole of Los Angeles.

She felt like a marine creature, a pilot fish, a dipper or darter around the perimeter of some animal greater and slower than herself. Or possibly not an animal but a planet, a distant body. The complainer seemed remote not only in space but in time, the progression of his hair, dark to white, a horizon of years. As though she crawled toward him across some time-lapse vastness, a desert or ocean floor which bloomed and declined before her eyes. Every darting movement she made, her whole lithe, slippery course across his body, the seeking effort of her mouth and hands, was an attempt to close this margin between them. But with no apparent malice or guile he'd shunted away, as though their exact proximity was polar, regulated by magnetic force.

She'd heard herself laughing and producing other noises which had no simple name, but hadn't spoken sentences in hours. Language had come out of the complainer, though. As before, when he'd muttered in his sleep. The same words, she was certain of it now.

"Carl?" Her own voice shocked her, restored her modesty slightly.

"Yes?"

"When you were coming did you say 'pour love on the broken places,' or was I just imagining it?"

"I said that, yes." He propped on his elbows.

"Over and over again under your breath."

"Yes."

"Why?"

"I guess I just needed something to say."

She began to see that all of what she felt, the strange abject yearning that had grown inside her through this journey to nowhere conducted across the two hotel beds, across this night turned to afternoon, might have a name. If he could say the word, why couldn't she? He'd asked her to keep it a secret, though, and she would. Her tenderness and awe, the risk of love, would be kept secret between her and herself.

She persisted with her question. "Where did it come from? Those particular words."

"I made it up."

"You couldn't have." She spoke tenderly, not wishing to disillusion him.

"Not just now, I mean. Before."

"I read the same words on a bumper sticker."

"You did?" He brightened.

"Yes."

"It's on T-shirts, too. And coffee mugs."

"Why?"

"That's my work. My latest. I'm the author of a line of slogans. Sometimes I can't get them out of my head."

"So it doesn't mean anything in particular that you were saying that while we made love?" It gave her a clandestine thrill to say the word aloud, as though releasing pressure in a covert orgasm or sneeze. He'd opened himself to her, despite these ridiculous explanations. She vowed to adore him wordlessly and perfectly. They'd discuss anything but what they really felt, the silently expanding center of the universe.

"When I've coined an itchy phrase it's all I can think about until I come up with another one."

"An itchy phrase?"

"That's what it's called, an itchy or gummy phrase."

"Tell me another one."

"Let's see. One of my favorites is 'All Thinking Is Wishful.' I had a good run with that a few years ago."

"What's a good run?"

"To make a good living I only have to come up with something as gummy as that every six months or so."

"What do you do the rest of the time?"

He widened his palms and made an apologetic face.

Here it was, at last. She'd discovered him, her fat man, her fat life. The complainer was like a house she didn't have to shrink to enter, a doorway she didn't have to turn sideways to pass through. To truly love someone was to make them feel ridiculous and free, she felt. The complainer's hair was white but he was more like a child than anyone she knew. She wondered if he knew what he had shown her: how it was possible to replace disappointment with astonishment.

"Are you hungry?" she asked.

In reply he turned his head and gnashed at her foot.

"There's a place I want to show you where they serve these great fish tacos."

What occurred after they'd checked out of the motel she couldn't reconstruct, except that he'd had to drive her car again, and that she'd given him her keys and told him the address of her apartment on Elsinore. She wondered, vaguely, whether they'd been seen by anyone she knew, either at the taco stand's parking lot or as they drove on Sunset, window cranked so she could rest her chin, doglike, on the passenger door's top and gulp cool air. By the time she gathered that the distant pastoral sound of trickling water was her own kitchen sink, where the complainer stood rinsing her blouse clean of flecks of what had begun rushing out of her in the Siete Mares parking lot, he'd already stripped her clothes, tucked her into bed on her couch, and pulled her shades against the day's light, which skewed in orange stripes over the couch and her bedspread. It might have been three or five or seven in the afternoon or evening. Lucinda's eyes ached, as though bruised from behind by the force of her stomach's expulsion of the food. She tremored within her blankets, impossibly happy.

"Carl?"

"You're awake again," he whispered, as though there were someone else to overhear.

"I wasn't asleep."

He drew near to examine her, perhaps less interested in her testimony than in the report of his own eyes.

"I puked because I'm in love with you," she said, trashing her vow.

"Sleep now."

"I'm not tired. I have to get up."

He placed his fingers to her lips, then tiptoed backward to the doorway, and was gone.

She was woken by the doorbell what might have been twenty or a thousand minutes later, bolting upright in her nest of blankets on the couch, measuring her disbelief that she was home, that she was alone, that he was gone. Maybe this was him, returned.

"Come in," she croaked.

Denise hustled in and shut the door behind her, her gaze mapping the scene in rapid evaluation.

"It's eight, Lucinda."

"Why is it eight?"

"It just is, that's all."

"I fell asleep. I mean, starting at an unusual time, I guess."

"I don't need an account of your movements," said Denise. "We're on at nine. I'll run the shower."

Naked and humbled, Lucinda tramped to a place beneath the steam, while the day's telephone messages—Denise, Falmouth, Matthew, Denise again—unspooled in the background, an epic of beckonings, censures, lengthening silences. Meanwhile, Denise shifted Lucinda's bass and amplifier through the door, to her car.

Lucinda charted Denise's progress as a series of scraping and rustlings as Denise negotiated the apartment's slanted concrete walkway, which was shrouded in overgrown jade and aloe. At last came a decisive slam of the car's trunk.

"Here." Denise wrenched off the hot water and offered a towel, hustling Lucinda along. "I laid out clothes."

For months Lucinda had auditioned in her closet for a first-gig wardrobe, the perfect art-band garb, precedent for a new public identity. She'd settled on nothing definite. Now she donned the brown corduroys and orange capped-sleeve T-shirt Denise had chosen, incapable of resisting a fate likely as good as any other.

"I guess I missed the sound check."

"It isn't only the sound check, Lucinda. Loading in and breaking down is part of being in a band. It isn't just, you know, the drummer's job."

"I'm sorry."

"It's okay," Denise sighed. "We were worried, that's all. Anyway, it was sort of anticlimactic, more of a no-sound check, really."

Lucinda wanted to explain, but couldn't begin. In a night and a day her world had parted into halves impossible to reconcile or even mention to each other.

Bedwin waited in Denise's passenger seat, so Lucinda clambered into the back, beside her instrument. "Where's Matthew?"

"At Jules Harvey's loft, with our stuff."

"Are you okay, Lucinda?" asked Bedwin.

"I'm fine, Bedwin. I'm just waking up from a really strange sleep and a very sudden shower."

"That sounds difficult."

"I'm terrific, really."

Lucinda leaned her head between Denise's and Bedwin's headrests, touched her fingers to their heads from behind, felt them tighten their shoulders to their seats, resisting her. If she couldn't confess the subject of her happiness she could try to infect them with it nonetheless. The complainer had shown her that her happiness was all one thing, an arrow running, for instance, through her delirious visitation of the two hotel rooms, through drink and talk and sex and food and sleep and even vomit. The arrow of her happiness pierced all those moments and this one as well, the arrival of her friends to whisk her to Falmouth's Aparty. The big moment that had come at last, come for them all. For Matthew, estranged from the human world and needing to be pulled back. For Denise, so fierce and nervous on the band's behalf. For Bedwin, their terrified genius, who'd written such excellent songs, though not without secret assistance from Lucinda and Carl. Which proved what she felt: that the source of her happiness was a stream through all their lives, a bass figure under all their music, even if she was its sole hearer. Her instrument, wedged stiffly in the seat beside her, never reproachful or impatient, only waiting for her to plug it in and plumb its wood-and-wire soul: she loved it too.

Lucinda touched Bedwin's and Denise's napes again, put her fingers in their hair, which, she noticed, was cut the same length, and equally amateurishly. Sometime since seeing her last Denise had hacked her red-hennaed bangs into something more Joan of Arcish. Maybe Lucinda should take a child's scissors to her own hair as well. Haircuts signified change, and she felt changed. Plus it would give the band a look.

"It's our legendary first gig," she said. "Robot Head in Mourning or whatever it turns out we're known as. Some grainy photograph from this night will appear in the booklet of the box-set retrospective of our entire career."

Denise and Bedwin said nothing. Denise drove intently out of the side street, onto Sunset.

"Be excited or something."

"I guess I'd be more excited if we were behaving a little more like a band right now," said Denise. "Also if we were playing aloud. That would probably make a difference in how I felt."

"Maybe we will, maybe we'll shock everyone by suddenly playing aloud—"

"Won't they all be wearing headphones?" said Denise.

"Well, yes."

"I think Denise was just trying to say that helping to move the equipment is an important aspect of being—"

"I told her already, Bedwin," said Denise.

Lucinda penitently lugged her own amp as the three band members filtered through the horde of the Aparty's invitees. The April night was clear and warm and smelled of lime and fir, like the desert's rim, the place you'd reach in a day if you walked east out of the city, which you'd never do. Distant wheeling spotlights grazed the sky west of Koreatown. Here, far-twinkling stars were visible, five or six of them at least. The Aparty's invitees massed at a rehabbed industrial building on Olympic Boulevard, whose freight elevator served as the undistinguished entrance to Jules Harvey's loft. They spilled into the street, arriving in bunches, a pedestrian explosion excited by the unlikeliness of itself. Lucinda saw faces she recognized. Mildred

Zeno, the painter, Matthew's previous ex. They had something in common now, Lucinda supposed, like former opponents traded to the same team. Gillian Unger, Lucinda's old cohort at the Coffee Chairs. Perhaps she still labored there, beneath the espresso steam. Meade Everdark, columnist for the *Echo Park Annoyance*, leaned his elbow on the roof of a parked Jeep, gesturing with animation as he proved some point to the passengers inside. Clay Howl and Richard Abneg, guitarist and drummer of the Rain Injuries, stood swapping heavy looks with someone who might be Bruce Wagner. John Huck offered a cigarette to Maud Winchester. Denied early entrance by Falmouth's rigid concept, they inaugurated festivities curbside instead, and gabbling and smoking scanned the crowd for their friends. They swapped earphones to sample one another's dance mixes, broke out bottles or joints they'd secreted on their persons, having rightly feared a dryish occasion upstairs. The steward from Ixnay produced stem glasses and stood doling red wine to a queue of art-school ingenues.

Falmouth's interns sighted the band members and shooed Apartygoers aside to open a path to the elevator's doors, two paint-blistered steel portals studded with rusty bolts. One intern rapped at the doors and they parted to reveal a wizened Asian man in a porkpie hat and suspenders, manipulating a brass-handled wheel with one hand while gripping a smoldering cigarette and a folded-over Korean newspaper in the other. He arched an eyebrow, grunted, and seized Lucinda's amp, brandishing his newspaper like a flyswatter to brush the curious throng back from the doors. The band followed him inside.

"Mr. Oo doesn't speak English but he knows Korean kung fu," Jules Harvey explained, bowing to usher them from the elevator at the seventh floor, the top. Harvey wore a forest-green three-piece suit with a zipper in place of its buttons. He still wore his Tigers cap and high-top sneakers, and gaped like a turkey through his frames. "I'm positive he could slay you with that newspaper." The tiny man had grabbed the amplifier and bass and now soldiered across the vast empty space of the loft toward the distant riser. There, Matthew sat alone in a small grove of their equipment, behind Denise's kit, tapping his fingers on her snare. The riser was unexpectedly high, and their unoccupied microphones and monitors looked persuasively professional from this angle, rescued from their rehearsal space.

The floor was a plain of polished wood, scattered with pillars, the ceiling a barren lid pressing low overhead, decorated with track lighting and a dingy, unlit mirror ball. The triangular loft formed a funnel pointing to the riser where the band would play, or mime playing. The prospects of the crowd downstairs fitting itself obediently inside seemed, to Lucinda, poor. Even if they could all squeeze up through the chute of the elevator, what chance they'd fall in line with Falmouth's commands? The interns scurried off now, presumably to find their leader. Lucinda, with Denise and Bedwin, followed. Crossing the open dance floor Lucinda felt exposed, a cat in a cathedral.

Jules Harvey scurried beside her, hands joined behind his back. "There isn't anything to be concerned about," he mused in his soft voice. "If we begin late it shouldn't compromise the underlying premise in any important sense."

"I wasn't concerned," said Lucinda. "We're ready whenever you like."

"I was thinking more of Falmouth."

"Is something wrong with Falmouth?"

"Perhaps after you greet your compatriots you'd be willing to follow me."

"Maybe we better go now."

Denise and Bedwin continued toward the stage, while Lucinda followed Harvey. Behind the elevator was hidden the loft's tiny kitchen and bathroom, and above, connected by a short spiral stair, nestled an elevated sleeping platform, with a ceiling so low Lucinda had to stoop. The melancholy living space was a mole's burrow, suggestive of Harvey's secret armpit-sniffer's despondency. "Will you remove your shoes, please?" said Harvey at the top of the stair. Lucinda crushed the backs of her sneakers with her toes, squeezing them off without untying the laces.

The scene had an air of private ritual. Falmouth knelt on Jules Harvey's futon, his knees surrounded by a heaped disarray of headphones and portable tape and disk players. Two shopping bags of additional equipment slumped unpromisingly on the floor. A gun nested in the cushions. Lucinda recalled something about a starter's pistol. She hoped it wasn't as real as it looked. The small shelf beside Jules Harvey's bed contained candles and two neat stacks of glossy magazines, possibly pornographic. The two interns sat coolly sharing a joint on a love seat in the corner. Their unspeaking presence seemed almost malevolent now, Falmouth's fantasy of a world decorated with servile girls gone sour.

Headphones clung crookedly to Falmouth's dome. Sweat trickling on his jaw, he stabbed buttons on a scuffed silver Walkman, then rolled his eyes and thrust the rig aside.

"Where have you been?" he said to Lucinda.

"I took a shower. What's wrong?"

"It's no good," he said. "Jules invited too many people and they didn't bring anything to listen to and when they all come upstairs they're going to destroy everything. We don't have enough tape players. Half of these don't work at all. We can't let them in, it's too many. Did you see?"

"I saw," said Lucinda. "It's half of Silver Lake."

"This happens," said Jules Harvey. "An invitation becomes exponential, something gets in the air. Suddenly it's the party everyone has to be at on a given night, the party of the season. We couldn't have foreseen how your list and mine would catalyze. People are afraid not to be at an event like this. Many others will eventually lie and claim they were."

"It wasn't meant to be a party," said Falmouth. "That's the problem. You threw a party."

"I'm sorry," said Jules Harvey. Steel flashed behind his usual gray tone of haplessness. "It's what I do." Lucinda understood that Harvey really was indomitable, the human equivalent of a cartoon turtle who appeared to plod ineffectually, yet when you tried to outrun him, turned up seated calmly on a log a few feet ahead of you, smoking a cigar and annotating a racing form with a stub of pencil.

Falmouth gestured for his interns, who didn't budge. "We'll be selective," he said. "I won't let them up without headphones."

"I'd prefer not to disappoint so many people," said Jules Harvey.

"What do you suggest, then?" said Falmouth.

"Let's have them up. We can feed and entertain them for a while. Get them on your side, Falmouth, then you can propose something. Here." Harvey reached across Falmouth's knees and plucked the pistol from the cushions. "One of you children handle this."

One of the interns nodded and stubbed out the joint, took the pistol from Harvey.

"It makes a very loud noise, so be careful. When you've got their attention, try to explain."

The intern nodded, and she and her companion moved to the spiral stair. Lucinda saw that some mysterious but unmistakable transfer had occurred. These were Jules Harvey's interns now.

When they were gone, Lucinda said, "I ought to go down and, uh, greet my compatriots."

Harvey spread his hands. "Maybe we should all go. We can leave this stuff up here for now."

Falmouth nodded disconsolately. The sacks of headphones and tape players seemed irrelevant now, the very medium of his great project demoted to "stuff."

"Do you want something to drink, Falmouth?" said Harvey.

"I'd like some water, please."

Lucinda led the other two downstairs. Denise and Bedwin hovered at the base of the stair. Jules Harvey led Falmouth into the kitchen and Denise told Bedwin, speaking as if to a child, "Go with them. I'm sure Jules can help you find something." Bedwin drifted in after Harvey and Falmouth, leaving Denise and Lucinda alone.

"There's an aura of doom around here," said Lucinda.

"I guess we all get to keep our day jobs," said Denise.

"By my count you're the only one who has one."

"Don't you work for Falmouth?"

"I don't see a big future for myself in complaints."

"We can all move into my apartment," said Denise. "We'll be one of those bands that's also a utopian collective, an experimental group marriage, and then we can all kill one another."

"Don't forget a certain, ahem, bathtub-dweller."

"There's room for everyone."

"What's Bedwin looking for, anyway?"

"He wants a stool for onstage. He said playing standing up makes him feel naked."

Falmouth came glaring from the kitchen, startling them. "Don't be so blatant with your mutinies," he said ferociously.

"What do you mean?"

"That you imagine I've fallen so low I'd accept the charity of living in the squalor of your band is disgusting enough. What I really can't fathom is how you awarded me the nickname 'bathtub-dweller.' "

The interns rematerialized, stopping Falmouth in his tracks. They stood like Shakespearian courtiers, waiting to deliver their report. Jules Harvey, apparently attuned to the young women by some deep wavelength, emerged from the kitchen and bowed at them to begin, ducking his baseball cap with Buddhist complacency.

"We failed," announced one of the interns. The other nodded, consenting that they spoke with one voice.

"Did you fire the gun?" asked Harvey.

"Yes. We fired the gun and opened a dialogue with what seemed like a reasonable faction."

"I'm surprised they don't yet have elected representatives," said Falmouth.

"It also helps that Mr. Oo had the fire extinguisher," the intern explained, ignoring Falmouth. "I think that got their attention more than the pistol."

"Fire extinguisher?"

"A contingent of sound poets had lit a bonfire between two parked cars. But Mr. Oo put it out."

"Go on."

"At a certain point negotiations broke down. They figured out there isn't anything to drink up here."

"That's not necessarily the case," said Harvey. "I always have a few bottles in reserve."

"You have to listen," insisted the intern. "They don't need us anymore. They intercepted your caterers. Someone leaked a rumor that the banquet wasn't going to be made available to the dancers. That isn't actually true, is it?"

Jules Harvey looked at Falmouth, who shrugged. Lucinda was impressed at Harvey's effect on the students. She'd never heard them speak so many words while in Falmouth's dominion.

"They're having a sort of tailgate party now," said the intern. "I think it's even bigger than before. A couple of the servers are friends of ours from school, as it happens. They're walking around with trays of chicken satay and tuna belly on rice crackers."

Jules Harvey scratched his chin and adjusted his spectacles, summoning his deepest resources. The rest of them stood twitching slightly, deferring to his turtle authority.

"Go back downstairs, but don't use the gun this time. What we want is more along the lines of a whispering campaign. Tell a select few that the band is about to start. Propose that they might want to get a good spot near the stage. You don't have to talk to strangers. Let the majority be curious. Mention it to those server friends of yours, especially if they're young and attractive."

"Should we say which band?"

"They don't have a name," said Falmouth bitterly.

"It's better that way. Just say the band is about to start. It implies that anyone would know which band it was, suggesting a reference to something already confirmed as desirable by others. That's why they're all here anyway."

"To see the band?" asked Lucinda, confused.

"No. I mean because most of them heard someone refer to 'that party everyone's going to tonight,' as if they should already know about it. Like 'that restaurant everyone goes to,' or 'that girl everyone's trying to date.' It's much better than anything specific." Harvey urged the interns to the elevator. "Go now. Falmouth, come help me open the windows."

"For jumping, I hope."

"I want them to hear."

"Hear what?"

"The band, of course. They'll have to play loud."

Lucinda understood now that her old friend had gone up against a force more profound than Jules Harvey. Falmouth's past works had involved manipulating people's despair, pensiveness, ennui. Those were malleable materials, lightly guarded by their possessors. The Aparty was another matter. Here, Falmouth had tried to appropriate other people's happiness, and been met with that property's devastatingly blithe resistance. Happiness was disobedient, had its own law. As a freshly minted local expert, Lucinda felt qualified to know.

---

**m**atthew sat on the riser's edge, taking the private interlude as an opportunity for tuning his guitar. For Matthew, Lucinda knew, this was a humbling ordeal, one which, like certain bodily functions, stood a better chance of being accomplished without witnesses. More than once at rehearsal he'd abandoned the effort and shamefacedly handed his guitar to Bedwin for adjustment. Lucinda felt a surge of tenderness. She almost wished they could leave Matthew alone there, not prick the bubble in which he dwelled, elegant as a black-and-white photograph of some legendary figure caught backstage. He'd shaved, trimmed his sideburns into neat wedges, donned a black turtleneck, shined his boots, made every attempt to retrieve himself from the kangaroo's slough his apartment had become and make himself ready for the band's unveiling. He'd be the last to know they were going to play aloud. Lucinda wanted to be the one to tell him.

Bedwin had found a step stool in Jules Harvey's kitchen. He placed it on the riser in the clear spot behind his monitor. Then Denise led him away, promising snacks, leaving Lucinda and Matthew with the equipment. Matthew offered her a hand up onto the riser. She accepted for the pleasure of the contact of their palms, his cool, hers hot. She was in a fever, her body an engine churning at toxins. Matthew reached out and brushed a lock of hair from her forehead. He spoke gently, as if he'd been the one to rouse her from the late-afternoon fugue on her couch.

"You have a wild happy look in your eyes."

"Denise seemed pissed that I missed the sound check."

"It mostly involved Falmouth criticizing our clothing."

"It might be more important than you think. Jules Harvey wants us to play. I mean, with sound coming out."

"What about Falmouth's important art?"

"It's still important in principle. But something more spontaneous decided to happen in actuality."

She rescued her bass from its fuzzy coffin, then moved to
plug in to her amp and begin tuning. She felt Matthew peering
at her, unbudged from his seat on the riser. She wondered if he'd
made himself pretty for her sake. She wondered if her provoca-
tions on the telephone, the kanga dootie song, had somehow
shifted him slightly in her direction again, as opposed to that
dim specter she'd encountered in the supermarket.

"Lucinda?"

"Yes?"

"I need to talk to you about the, uh, marsupial situation."

"I owe you an apology."

"I don't care about that," he said, with a warmth and sincerity that instantly absolved her of both break-in and phone call. "I
need your help."

"Yes?" She felt her breath catch, slightly.

His eyes grew shy. "Maybe this isn't the right time."

"Anytime," she said.

"Tomorrow, let's talk tomorrow."

"Yes."

Denise and Bedwin returned, Bedwin with both hands
around a sardine sandwich. They'd been consulting with the interns, who now scuttled across the great empty room in the
direction of Jules Harvey's kitchen.

"Jules wants us to start in five minutes," said Denise. "We
need a set list." She unfolded a sheet of paper and smoothed it
against the riser's plywood, then uncapped a marker and waved
the others to kneel beside her.

"Start with 'Monster Eyes,' " said Lucinda.

"We'd play it to an empty room," said Denise. "All they'll hear from the street is the bass line."

Matthew said, "So let's pick something that'll sound good from the street. Something loud that we don't care about, like 'Hell Is for Buildings' or 'Crayon Fever.'"

"I don't want to play 'Crayon Fever' at all," said Denise. "We can't start with something old and depressing. We have to inspire ourselves."

"'Dirty Yellow Chair,'" suggested Bedwin.

Denise wrote it in block letters at the top of the page.

"We're wasting that as the first song, too," said Lucinda.

"No, she's right," said Matthew. "We need to hear ourselves sound good."

"Then 'The Houseguest,'" said Bedwin, pointing a finger at the blank space where Denise's marker circled in the air. They all looked at Bedwin, who only chewed his fish sandwich noisily. This new task of constructing a set list might rightly belong to their auteur.

"What about 'Temporary Feeling' next?" said Denise, looking to Bedwin now.

"Mmmm, 'Astronaut Food,' then 'Temporary Feeling,'" said Bedwin. The others nodded, as though hurrying to board a vehicle that might depart without them. The sequence of songs began to feel inevitable in the manner of language or music itself, as though Bedwin were revealing to them a hidden grammar embedded in the band's motley offerings.

"Right, sure, there'll be an audience by the time of 'Astronaut Food,'" said Denise. Lucinda imagined the drummer was anticipating their showpiece, the two women harmonizing on the single microphone.

"Why not 'Monster Eyes' after 'Temporary Feeling'?" asked Matthew.

Bedwin nodded, and Denise jotted it down.

" 'Secret from Yourself,' " said Lucinda, captivated now.

" 'Hell Is for Buildings.' "

" 'Sarah Valentine.' "

" 'Nostalgia.' "

" 'Canary.' "

"Maybe hold 'Actually Quite Funny' for a first encore?"

"What about 'Tree of Death'?"

They called out the names eagerly, unafraid of mistakes. Denise wrote nothing down without Bedwin's oracular consent. In this manner the set list was hashed out.

t he first chords, chunks of noise, rebound in the gulch of buildings. They seem, to those on the sidewalk, an atonal clatter, one unrelated to the tick and throb of drum and bass which had reached them independently, conveyed an instant before through the curb to their calves and knees, perhaps even as high as their genitals. Soon, though, the listeners' ears wrangle the dissonant sounds into sensible conjunction, a kind of on-the-spot reconstruction of this music's sense in the first place. Any listener schooled in the form could peel it off echoing architecture as easily as resolve it through a radio's static. Those staticky growls were, sure, amplified guitars, echoing in the cage of the drumbeat. Vocals, too, though distorted by the street's reverb effect a general drift was discernible, twice through a verse, building to a chorus: hey, everyone knows how this works, knows it in their bones, even if unable to articulate it exactly: rock 'n' roll. It's what makes this band sound alike to any other that makes them intriguing, at this distance: they could be the Beatles, heard from the street. Or, just as easily, the Beards. The crowd buzzes with the general sense that an obscure evening has located its raison d'être. At least you'd have to go upstairs to know. Whoever they were, they were playing live, and you, on the sidewalk with skewered Thai chicken in your hand, are missing the set. Anyway, you were curious to see what this famous party loft was about after all, despite the spontaneous curbside revel's rude charms.

The band concluded their opener's last chorus just as Mr. Oo levered open the freight elevator doors and the first clutch of guests spilled onto the floor. Someone—Jules Harvey? the appropriated interns?—had located a master control panel for the loft's lighting, and fiddled until the stage was encircled with a blobby series of wide purplish spots from a track of lamps mounted behind the band, angled to glare in the eyes of anyone standing near enough to discern the band's faces, and casting the floor between stage and elevator into dark. Without footlights to provide underlighting, the band appears mysteriously remote, silhouettes draped in indigo as they confer with one another and their set list, nodding, perhaps mumbling a word or two, but inaudible above the low crackle and drone of speakers broadcasting nothing but their own electronic readiness, at top volume. A female voice, the drummer's, counts "One, two, three, four," and the second song is launched, with a single rim shot like a firecracker, igniting the guitarist. He's a feeble figure, hunched atop a tall stool, and apparently unable to play without watching his fingers, but who now lays out an unexpectedly slablike power chord, stretching a sneakered toe from where it had been curled inside a spoke of his stool to trigger a distortion pedal on the stage floor.

"The Houseguest" is a weirdly grim number, a defiant tirade by a guest wronged by his hosts, over a set of changes that might be the billionth rewrite of some three-chord chestnut, "You Really Got Me," say, or "Twentieth Century Fox," but played with conviction and vigor by the band, who associate the song, one of their earliest, with the uncovering of their own capacity to join in birthing ferocious noise. No one's ever quite dared to query the guitarist, who delivered this lyrical concept to the band whole formed, on its source; no one ever will. The song's a confidence builder for the singer, who finds that it liberates some element of rageful self-pity his own temperament usually quashes. He loves twisting his body as he bellows the raw quatrain that fits into a gap of feedbacky silence between the rolling changes:

*I'm the house GUEST*
*I can't get no REST*
*In your guest BED*
*I'll sleep when I'm DEAD*

The moment he's delivered the word "dead" the singer's voice is drowned in the band's wave again. Though he'll go on enunciating the houseguest's complaint, these are the sole words a listener could distinguish with any confidence, and certainly the only ones that matter. The singer's altered by them into a performer with a series of false faces to wear, urgent charades to put across. The band feels this, and it's one reason the song is an unquestioned favorite. Tonight the band's audience feels it too.

For that's what they've become, in the space of a song: an audience. Drinks or cigarettes in hand, in bunches of two and three and four, unused Walkmans clipped to their belts or shoved in a purse, attentive to the band or babbling at conversations uninterrupted from their beginnings on the sidewalk, acquaintances of Falmouth's and Harvey's, journalists from local weeklies, art collectors, disc jockeys, graduate students, catering staff, an uncertain few who'd called the complaint line in the past week and been enlisted to the Aparty by Falmouth's interns, curious seekers who'd received no invitation at all, even a few who'd spontaneously stopped their cars to see what the fuss was about—all had meandered together into a single entity, one massed along the periphery of purple light that covered the stage, and scattering from that front toward the kitchen, where Harvey and the interns now splashed together vodka and mixers, just to keep the atmosphere up. The party had become a show. It had never even considered being a conceptual art piece. It never would.

Without pause the band's into "Astronaut Food." On this number, more melodic and inviting than the previous, the women in the band make a bid to usurp the singer's spotlight, and about a hundred men watching ask themselves why they've never had the eyes before to see they ought to have asked the drummer or the bassist on a date. Jubilantly singing into the single microphone the two women look fresh and alive, a thousand percent less ordinary than at the retail outlets or previous social gatherings from which these men are fairly certain they recognize them. As if sensing this shift, the singer glares at the audience between verses, daring them to presume in their dawning hunger for the figures onstage. This, in turn, is sensed by and thrills the women, who seem in a way to be taunting the singer behind his back.

This band's got something, and some of the something they've got is the allure of an enclave at odds within itself and yet impenetrable to others, its members exchanging small gestures of disaffection within their troupe that makes others crave to be included in the fond dissension.

"Temporary Feeling" is quieter, in a way that disseminates silence in the room, chatterers and gabblers at the loft's edges hushed by the effort of those nearer to the band who strain to follow the lyric. As far as anyone can make out it's an intimate tale, in murmured passages of unrhymed lyric, prose stanzas which might or might not be the singer's own confession, pages exported from a journal. Another magic spell this band trades in is the mystery of authorship: If a heart's revealed here, whose? If a famous conceptual artist is putting on this show, should something about this band be taken to be in quotation marks? Is this band a stalking horse? Is the song a fiction, or a cover version, or the lament of someone hiding in plain sight? Who's moving that mouth?

Seeded with quiet, the crowd hears itself exhale between the waning final chord of "Temporary Feeling" and the advent of their own clapping. This first full and unembarrassed burst of applause marks a threshhold in the audience's belief that tonight's performance is no accident but the event they'd come here to witness in the first place. It's into the face of this loose barrage of cheers and whistles that the four members of the band, not pausing to mutter "Thank you" or to revel in praise they'd be petrified to believe they'd earned, serves forth, with a drum kick and a bass thrum and a chiming guitar figure, the instantly legible hook of their next song.

The song is "Monster Eyes," and it comes set to make an impression. For band and audience alike, the evening finds its watershed, dividing Before from After. In the audience's case, the watershed divides the perfectly agreeable songs they can no longer quite remember from the one they'll go out humming, the one that causes everyone, during its third chorus or through the howl of cheers that erupt in its wake, to lean into someone's ear and bark through cupped hands, "These guys are good!" or "I love this song!" The rest of the band's set will unfold as confirmation: the audience has seen and celebrated something, and is entitled to feel special for having done so. Jules Harvey has done it again. Or Falmouth Strand. You weren't sure what anything had to do with anything else, but cool people were certainly involved. You weren't wrong to come out tonight. You'd found yourself right in the thick of something. You had to be there, *the night they first played "Monster Eyes,"* and you were.

For the band, this first public rendition of what's instantly become their hit song is the moment when time stops its hectic flow and earth's atmosphere expands, just a little, to make room for something new, embodied by themselves. It's the moment when they realize that rather than being as good as they'd always hoped, or even better than they hoped, they're simply as good as they *are*, no hope required. Enshrined behind the even newer songs—"Dirty Yellow Chair," "Secret from Yourself," and the others resulting from the sheaf of titles Lucinda presented in Bedwin's apartment—"Monster Eyes" no longer seems, to the band, in any important sense new. It's a fixture in their lives, a given. They can't remember where it came from because the truth is that the song was there all along, waiting to be given the air, allowed to breathe. The song represents the band's nature impatiently asserting itself: here's what we sound like, already!

The rest of the set is gravy. The audience rolls over for the grinding, staticky "Hell Is for Buildings," which the guitarist furls right into the cheers for "Monster Eyes," as though to urge the band past any possible complacency. "Secret from Yourself" goes over too, the singer animating the lyrics with Kabuki theatricality, making them a remonstration of the audience's own failings, then forgiving them, barely, in the final verse. "Canary in a Coke Machine" makes light relief, gets a little sloppy and lets everyone off the hook. Then "Shitty Citizen" and "Nostalgia Vu," which build in their way rather nicely to "Actually Quite Funny," which had become, while nobody was looking, a show closer. Afterward there's no place to hide during the applause and shouting for more, no curtain to drop, no backstage, though singer and bassist do step to one side while the guitarist sits nodding on his stool and the drummer mumbles "Thank you" several times into her mike. Someone—Jules Harvey? the interns?—locates the light switches again and kills the purple spots, so the band is left represented by the connect-the-dot glow of their equipment's power indicators, while the vibrating crowd is illuminated only by the answering glows of their cigarette tips and the oceanic moonlit blue leaking through the windows. Into this dark the crowd roars. Then lights come back up, and bassist and singer scoot back to their places.

What's left for an encore? First, "Sarah Valentine," if only because it would have broken their hearts not to play it. The other three members suspect the song of being prehistoric, some acoustic ballad the guitarist penned in high school and smuggled into their company. Tonight, who cares? The singer dips his mike stand to where the guitarist sits on his stool and the embarrassed guitarist warbles the last chorus, possibly a future ritual invented on the spot. Then, the song finished, someone in the crowd yells out "Monster Eyes" in the thick of the cheering. Other voices laugh recognition, and the cheering grows louder. The band members meet eyes and accept a plan without speaking, the guitarist mutters "Thank you" now as the familiar chords strike up again. Those two words being the only words the band has spoken from the stage all night, and now it's too late to adorn them, let alone to banter. Apparently they were to be the taciturn sort of band, who knew?

They play it again. It's a victory lap, now that there's nothing left to prove, no hard sell to put across. Doing so, they tear down the room once more, ensuring the crowd will dissolve into the night buzzing with the intoxication of this song. The second time, the listeners have begun to parse the lyrics, take them to heart—hey, this song's about you and me and the dangerous way we feel sometimes! It's about all of us! But it's about me most of all, each listener thinks. It's most particularly about dangerous me.

Now there's no clamor for a further encore. The band's played their perfect song for a second time, leaving nothing to wish for except disappointment, and who wishes for that? So, with no way to celebrate without getting silly, as the unseen hand behind the purple spotlights now shifts a single white spot to the mirror ball and the room is spangled, silly's what the crowd gets. Old imperatives, seemingly shrugged aside by the tyrannical revelers, are now revived. Those who brought along headphones and tape players don them and begin dancing asynchronously in the zone before the stage, one guy with a crew cut and his eyes squeezed closed doing a James Brown strut, a woman with orange bangs and headphones big as earmuffs sliding across the floor as though shuttling on some great invisible loom. The interns move through those on the fringes of the dance offering the shopping bags full of tape players and headsets, making more than a few converts, though massing everywhere are dozens upon dozens of celebrants who'd never understood what was expected of them in the first place. These others fall to babbling, eating and drinking, and mocking the dancers. It's Falmouth's Aparty, sort of. No one's quite so apart as Falmouth might have envisioned, and the artist himself may well have quit the scene in disgust.

The band's not forgotten. The gathering seems specially arranged to leave their set ringing in listeners' ears, nothing intruding on the echo of their chords but laughter and conversation and the mute, foolish dancing. Most feel it would be uncool to throng the band with an overt show of congratulations, so the four are left free to pack instruments and compare impressions, in their attempt to believe what's occurred, the version of themselves that's newly sprouted into existence. The band's hardly oblivious, though, to the awestruck or lustful gazes of nearby audience members. Someone in range of their hearing indulges in a pretentious explication of the band's influences. Another voice can be heard trying to sing the chorus of their momentous song. And the band will hardly be left to themselves for long. Wending through the mass of ecstatic dancers are several presences, calculating watchers on whom the band has made an impression. An evening like this brings them out of the woodwork.

they spoke in fragments, giving blundering accounts of what they'd felt onstage.

"You were so hot on 'Canary'—"

"I was just listening to Matthew."

"But I've never heard you play like that."

"Did I skip a verse of 'Nostalgia'?"

"Sure, but who cares?"

"We've never played 'Shitty Citizen' so fast."

"It sounded good."

"It sounded great. You finally really played a solo in that break, Bedwin."

"I just sort of suddenly knew what to do. I was waiting."

"You picked a good time to figure it out."

Denise began to twist apart her kit. Matthew and Lucinda, taking her cue, began winding cord. Bedwin sat rubbing his eyes, as though he'd watched too much television or was trying to believe or disbelieve a dream. It dawned on them only gradually that their eggshell of privacy had been pierced. When no one was looking the lip of the stage had been approached by men of guile and influence, unyouthful men in youthful clothes. The impresario in his baseball cap and zipper jacket, Jules Harvey, flanked by two others, one in jeans and a cowboy shirt and a small gold earring, the other wearing an ostentatiously rumpled brown corduroy suit, each with immaculately trimmed sideburns. The newcomers matched Harvey's rabbity intensity. They pitched forward on the balls of their feet as they waited for an introduction, eyes drilling side to side as if to defend their territories.

Behind them stood another man, older than the rest, and taller—taller even than Matthew—with a rocket of stone-white hair topping through a wide, scarflike headband. He bore a galactically sad, houndish expression on his eroded-cliff features, patiently waiting his turn. And too, floating through the crowd was yet another figure, one Lucinda would have recognized if she'd sighted him. She hadn't, yet. The band gave an audience to the phalanx at the stage's edge.

"You're a very hard band to see," said the man at Harvey's left, the one in corduroy. He grinned and thrust his hand at Matthew. "Very off the map, in a manner of speaking."

Matthew took his hand.

"It's always an interesting sign when music people get mixed up with art people. There's a good track record there. I can think of at least three or four very interesting examples that have made certain people who will go unnamed tremendously useful sums of money."

"We're not really mixed up with art people," said Matthew. "We just did this one gig as a favor to Falmouth. We're more our own thing."

"That's the spirit," said the corduroy man. "Listen, in the next days, even in the next five minutes, a lot of people are going to be trying to shake this hand that I'm shaking, and I just hope you'll recall I was first. Rhodes Bramlett. Considerable Records."

"We should get going," said Denise, tapping Matthew on the shoulder with a drumstick, offering fake smiles to the men at the edge of the stage. "Nice meeting you."

"I'd like to be in touch in the next few days," said Rhodes Bramlett, in a kindly, seeking tone. "Who would I be getting in touch with if I was?"

"We'll find you," said Denise. "Now we're leaving."

"Of course," said Jules Harvey. "But let me introduce you to another friend of mine. Mick Felsh, this is Monster Eyes."

"That's not our name," said Lucinda.

"No, of course," said Harvey amiably. "What is your name? As your de facto manager, I ought to know."

"We don't have one," said Denise. "And you're not our de facto anything."

"Pretty good name for a band, though," said Bedwin to himself.

"No name, I like that," said Mick Felsh, the man in the cowboy shirt. His voice was disarmingly nasal and high, a non sequitur to his garb. He spoke as if Bramlett of Considerable, inches away, were in fact a figment of a distant universe, impossible to perceive. "You people don't need me to tell you this, but that was a dynamite set." Felsh offered his hand to Denise, perhaps making a quick calculation of who among the players ought to be solicited, perhaps only hoping to put a brake on their departure. "I was telling Jules I'd love to help you guys demo some of that material. No need to worry about any kind of contract or commitment if it makes you guys uncomfortable. Just get into my studio and see how it feels. Get a document of the set you're playing these days, sort of Monster Eyes circa now, before anything changes, because you'd be surprised."

"Nothing's going to change," said Denise. "Except we're going to get better."

"It could be fun to record some demos, though," said Matthew.

"I wouldn't do anything without—" began Bramlett.

"One copy of the master," countered Felsh, his hand raised like a Boy Scout's. "You take it out the door with you."

"Doesn't matter, since we're not ready," said Denise. "Lucinda, help Bedwin pack up his stuff." Bedwin was ground to a halt, sat dope-eyed on his stool in the midst of their mike stands and cable. Lucinda tried to rouse herself but fell slack. She'd succumbed to a tidal exhaustion, the accumulated physical insult of too much joy, too many fish tacos and bass notes and orgasms flying in and out of her boundaries.

"We could all go sit upstairs," said Jules Harvey. "Just take a few minutes to talk. These moments don't come so often."

"Nah, we're in a hurry," said Denise.

"Where are we in a hurry to?" asked Matthew.

"Yes, where are you going?" said Harvey. "This party's hardly over."

"To a place where bands go after gigs," said Denise. "A secret destination, known only to bands."

Now the tall man with the headband full of white hair and the mournful craggy face loomed into view, nudging Mick Felsh aside effortlessly, without seeming to notice the smaller man. He was dressed in a long, battered peacoat, missing buttons. He stood with his hands deep in its pockets as though braced against some arctic wind. He placed himself before the band and smiled and shook his head, mouth parted as if to speak, none of the sorrow banished from his eyes.

"Okay," he said finally. His voice rumbled, thrummed.

"Hey, I know you," said Matthew. "You're Fancher Autumn-breast."

"Yes."

"I've been listening to you since I was a kid," said Matthew.

Fancher Autumnbreast closed his eyes, shook his head again, sighed. "Sure, sweetheart."

"Nice to meet you," said Denise, nudging Matthew again. "Let's go."

"No, you don't understand," said Matthew. "Fancher Autumnbreast, from KPKD. *The Dreaming Jaw*."

"What's *The Dreaming Jaw*?"

"His midnight radio show, for like the last thousand years." Matthew didn't disguise his impatience. "He's fairly important, if you care anything about the history of music in this town."

"Let alone if you want to make some," added Jules Harvey.

"When I was a child I pretty much just wanted to be you," said Bedwin to Autumnbreast, so softly he was barely heard.

"Look." Autumnbreast ignored Bedwin, Denise, Harvey, anyone else, removed one gnarled, elegant hand from the peacoat's pocket and pushed a single finger against Matthew's chest. "Find me. You'll play your song. On the *Jaw*. Live in studio."

"Which song?"

"You know, babykins."

Fancher Autumnbreast turned and threaded through the chaotic, musicless dance floor. Jules Harvey and Mick Felsh and Rhodes Bramlett all stared and watched him go, as did the band. Autumnbreast left in his place a conspicuous vacancy, an authority gap.

Denise spoke first. "Let's just take the guitars. Jules, if you're supposed to be our manager now, you can make sure nobody screws with our equipment. Bedwin, guitar to the elevator, now. Matthew too. We'll break down when the party's out of the way, tomorrow maybe."

"Your equipment is safe," said Harvey, bowing. Felsh and Bramlett bowed too, not wishing to seem ungracious. Denise had won this round, it appeared. But she'd named Harvey as their manager, in front of the others. Perhaps he'd act as if authorized to speak for them. Word might even spread, by the same osmosis that had launched the evening in the first place.

Obeying Denise, Matthew seized up Lucinda's bass as well as his own guitar and started for the elevator. Bedwin too. Perhaps they hoped for another passing encounter with their hero, Fancher Autumnbreast. Denise pushed the cymbals and kicks she'd already partially broken down into some rough order. Lucinda slid off the stage.

At that moment he moved within the perimeter of lights and revealed himself. The complainer. Carl, Carlton. He stood in his same loose pants and untucked shirt covering the blunt hairy fact of his body, and gazing at her with his droll handsome disheveled look, his gone-to-seed glamour. He'd been there, surely, throughout the show. Had seen them play.

The band had discovered itself onstage like Helen Keller, connecting at last the idea or name for a thing to the thing itself, a blundering into a new world they'd never dared to name. At the same time another world had uncovered itself to Lucinda when she made herself drunk and naked for the complainer. Now they weren't two worlds, but one. It was all too much, he was too much for her, standing so patiently at the stage.

"The way you play that instrument makes me think of the way you fuck, if you don't mind my saying that."

"I don't mind," she said. "It's a bass."

"I mean to say very beautifully and forcefully."

"Thank you."

"With great sincerity and even with what I'd be tempted to call originality, if I didn't think originality was a word people throw around a lot without knowing what they're talking about."

"Uh, thank you."

"Because to really judge the originality of something you'd have to be familiar with all the possible precedents and sources, which very few people are ever likely to be."

"I'm not completely sure I understand."

"I couldn't help feeling I was listening to myself."

Lucinda examined him for signs of anger, found none. His words had been delivered with perfect cheer, as eloquent and seductive as if he'd been pouring them into her ear on the telephone in that time so long past, that telephonic life which felt now like a distant journey, recollected in postcards.

"How did you know to come here?"

He shrugged. "Someone on the complaint line suggested I come to this unusual dance party they were planning. One of the other receptionists, you weren't there that day. Then I saw a notice in the paper that the famous complaint guy was putting on a performance piece at this loft. It wasn't that hard to guess you'd be here, though the show was a surprise."

"Falmouth is my friend." She wanted him to know her life completely now. If he'd recognized the song lyrics and wasn't angry there might be nothing to hide. She'd let her new worlds be joined. She wanted him to know Falmouth and the others, was impatient that it all even needed explaining. That Falmouth and Matthew were, technically, her exes was a minor note. The complainer, of all people, would understand.

"I felt like if I squinted I could practically see myself onstage."

There might be something mildly autistic in the complainer's reactions, a flatness to the face with which he addressed the world. His stance toward hotels and automobiles and women's bodies, his cataloging of her orgasms, his deafness to social pretense, all had a strangely equable quality. It made Lucinda love him more, not less. He crossed the grain of ordinary life, deliriously indifferent.

"I used your words as lyrics," she blurted.

"I noticed."

"Bedwin wrote the music. The guitarist."

"Does he know?"

She shook her head, wide-eyed. "Nobody knows."

She pushed away from the stage, nearer to him.

"I usually collect hundreds, if not thousands, per verb or noun."

"I don't have my checkbook."

"I'll take a hostage."

The complainer reached his hand into her hair, cradling her skull. She kissed him, on tiptoe, felt the grit of his unshaved cheek. She found herself folded into his encyclopedia of clothes and hair and limbs. His free paw bridged her buttocks and drew her higher into the embrace. In the kiss Lucinda tasted traces of their night and afternoon, hints of herself or the Ambit's mustard and ketchup unrinsed from his face.

Someone tapped her shoulder. She turned and found the two appropriated interns standing unexpectedly close. They didn't speak, but like spectral sentinels nodded to indicate Denise, who waited a few yards from the stage, her rack toms tucked beneath one arm. Lucinda nodded and Denise lowered her head and moved through the dancers, for the elevator.

"I have to go be with the others."

"The others in the band."

"Yes."

"Can I come?"

She stared, not understanding.

"I've never been in a band before," he said.

She capped his mouth with her hand to silence him and to keep herself from kissing him again before the lingering interns. Then, helplessly, mouthed the back of her own hand instead, as though seeking him through prison bars. "Call me tomorrow," she whispered through her fingers. "Or tonight." Then escaped.

d enise hadn't lied, Tang's Donut was a place bands went to celebrate and debrief after shows. The others recognized this at once. Though by the standard of most gigs they'd played the Aparty ludicrously early, at Tang's it might as easily have been four in the morning. Traffic buzzed past on Sunset and Fountain, isolating Tang's like a reef in time. Elderly chess opponents in vintage suits nudged pawns across squares at their booths, under clicking, humming fluorescent fixtures, as though installed there by some miraculous hand that had plucked them from a 1930s Vienna kaffeehaus. Trays of cold congealed muffins lay untouched and unloved within the fingerprint-layered lead-glass cases, while the customers invariably queued for the same buttermilk doughnuts, dough flash-fried in irregular clumps with a browned horny crust, which gave way to the peachy-yellow fluff inside, too hot to eat if you badgered the drowsy, indifferent counterman to serve you from the cooling racks in the kitchen behind him.

Crowded at their booth, they juggled steaming buttermilk-dough fragments between fingers and lips, gobbling them when they could stand to. Here, it turned out, was why you wanted to play a triumphant gig: in order to eat Tang's doughnuts afterward. True, you could come here after merely seeing some other band play. They'd all done that. So, you sought glory then in order not only to sit at Tang's but to feel you deserved to. Denise slurped peppermint tea, made from Tang's hot water and a tea bag she'd stashed in her jacket, while Matthew, in vegetarian solidarity with his secret captive, sipped orange juice. Lucinda, heedlessly, drank coffee. Bedwin, hot chocolate.

"I feel like we left some opportunities back there," said Matthew.

"Those people only dug us because there are women in the band," said Denise. "They see it as some kind of marketing hook."

"We don't know that for a fact," said Matthew. "Anyway, it's not like that with Fancher Autumnbreast. He's got nothing to gain."

"Anyone who likes us already likes us for the wrong reasons," said Denise. "We've only ever played one set."

"A lot can happen in one set," said Lucinda. They fell silent in contemplation of it. The performance fizzed inside them like carbonation, the bubbles destined to unbind, bob to the surface, expire. Perhaps that was even what they'd come here for. Tang's was a sort of detox ward, a safe zone in which the band could decant, settle back into the safety of their familiar, unfamous lives.

"We sort of got a manager tonight," said Bedwin. He dunked a chunk of doughnut deep into his hot chocolate, displacing the liquid to the rim and nearly over.

"Maybe a name, too," said Matthew. He'd crumbled his own doughnut to fragments and spread the fragments around his place mat, wrecking his cake like his bathroom stowaway had wrecked her salad.

"That can't be our name," said Lucinda, a little panicked at all she knew and couldn't say. "It's a song. It can't be both a song and a band."

"Why not?" said Bedwin.

"It's stupid. Who does that?"

"Hey hey we're the Monkees," said Bedwin.

"That only proves my point."

"Black Sabbath has a song called 'Black Sabbath.'"

"I don't want that to be the name." Lucinda resisted speaking the famous phrase itself, as if to do so were to invoke the band's occult debt. She wanted the phrase to be smothered in silence, made a footnote. Never mind that it was the title of their hit. They'd write more that were better, leave "Monster Eyes" in the dust. Only Bedwin had any reason to suspect her, but he showed no sign he recalled that the lyrics originated outside himself. Her deception was as safe with him as it would be with a cat or a dog.

Lucinda was the band's invisible betrayer and its invisible angel at once. Ward of their innocence, she'd inserted the complainer's language into their art like LSD slipped into a punch bowl. Now she must persuade them that the effects were natural, that though the world had transmuted around them, the hallowed unit of the band remained untouched. Lucinda would take the crime on herself. The others would never know. She only needed to control the whims of the complainer, the least controllable person she'd ever encountered.

"Are We Not Men, We Are Devo," continued Bedwin. "'Clash City Rockers.' 'Give It to the Soft Boys.' And the Verlaines have a song whose whole chorus is just the word 'Verlaine' over and over again."

"That's enough, Bedwin," said Denise. She placed a quarter of her doughnut onto a napkin and pushed it, like a raft with humanitarian cargo, across to Bedwin, who'd been eyeing hers after gobbling his own.

"Our manager is an armpit sniffer," said Lucinda despondently. The four again fell silent, unsure how to encompass this remark.

"I do that," said Bedwin eventually.

"I mean other people's armpits," said Lucinda.


t he phone rang and Lucinda slugged to the pillow's edge. She stretched the receiver from its cradle to her head, which was too ponderous to raise from its nest. The receiver, too, was too heavy to hold, so she rested it on her face.

"Hello?"

"You awake?" asked Matthew.

"What time is it?" She'd been fathoms deep, possibly dreaming of the complainer, but the phone's chime had shattered any dreams, her first eyeful of daylight sweeping the remains off like motes on its beams. But it should have been the complainer calling, she felt.

"Ten," said Matthew. "Can we talk?"

"Marsupial predicament?"

"Yes."

"Come in half an hour."

She allowed her eyes to sag again for what seemed an instant. When she reopened them and padded into her kitchen she found Matthew there, having used his key. Or perhaps she'd left it unlocked. He scrounged in her refrigerator, hip-deep into the appliance. She stretched her T-shirt around her knees and peered over his shoulder. He rattled at back layers of condiments, prying at shrunken fists of tinfoil, artifacts she hadn't examined in months.

"You won't find anything in there," she said. "I fed it all to a fugitive yak who lives in my hamper."

"I'm broke," said Matthew. "Will you buy me breakfast?"

"Sure, but I have to go to the gallery. Falmouth owes me a paycheck. I'll put pants on."

Matthew didn't turn to see. "If you feel like it," he said, sucking a glob of something, peanut butter or chèvre, from his finger. "Uck."

They took Matthew's Mazda, with its moonroof open. A tape Lucinda had heard a hundred times before squeaked in the deck, a mix of bands from New Zealand and Australia that Matthew collected on vinyl like holy relics from another realm. Sunset Boulevard blazed, empty, rinsed in sunshine, the stray cars like bugs streaming in the footprint of a vast lifted rock.

"Where is everyone?" said Lucinda, shielding her eyes from the glare. "Is it some kind of holiday?"

"Saturday."

"Where are all the people?"

"In bed, like you usually are."

"Don't you have any other music?"

"The tape's stuck in the player."

Falmouth was at his desk the morning after the debacle, seeking consolation in routine. The gallery office was shuttered against the day's light, Falmouth's face lit by the blue-toned screen as he attacked his e-mail. Falmouth was the first person Lucinda knew to use it. It might have been his invention, an art-

work he'd tricked the world into adopting, the true Aparty.
Lucinda stood beside him and cleared her throat. Matthew hung
back, never happy to visit the gallery.

"Boss, I need some money."

Falmouth looked up, scowling. "Didn't you people get some
sort of signing bonus last night? Isn't a number-one record worth
anything anymore?"

"We'll reimburse you out of our first royalties."

"No, you'll waste it all on cocaine and prostitutes, because
that's what rock stars do."

"Just enough for breakfast."

"This is severance pay. You're all fired. I had an epiphany last
night. The world of complaints can carry on without my help. It
has a certain inexorable momentum. Frankly, I'm not sure it
needed me in the first place." Falmouth's gallery had a crest-
fallen air, Lucinda saw now. An enterprise that teetered on despondency, it had been restrained from that brink by Falmouth's
will, a gambler's bluff. Today the place felt vacated, rustling with
ghosts of spectators moved elsewhere, to the next curiosity.

"You already fired me the other day," she said gently.

"That was different, that was affectionate."

"In retrospect this will be affectionate too."

"You're losing me." Falmouth waved his hand. "You know
what I would like? For someone to take me to breakfast every
once in a while."

"You want to come to breakfast?" said Lucinda, surprised,
glancing at Matthew. Yet perhaps Falmouth was innocent of the
grudge.

"I'll still pay," Falmouth said, almost begging now.

"Matthew and I have things to discuss," she began.

"Your future recording career under the hand of Jules Harvey," suggested Falmouth, his voice withering.

"I don't even want to hear that name today," said Lucinda.

"Come along," said Matthew. "I don't have any secrets."

Falmouth climbed past the passenger seat, into the back of Matthew's Mazda, another astonishment on this first morning after the Aparty. Falmouth ordinarily piloted his own car to any rendezvous, refusing passenger status even in a front seat. Now he sat dreamily trapped in Matthew's two-door, seated on a cushion leaking yellow foam, his shoes topping a heap of rubbish. The backseat had likely been the kangaroo's transport, though Falmouth had no way of knowing that. Oddly childlike, he rubbed at the five o'clock shadow on the back of his head and blinked at the street as though seeing it for the first time.

"What about that place that makes that great oatmeal frittata?" he said. "With the strawberries and cottage cheese on top."

"Hugo's, you mean?" said Matthew.

"Yes, that's it."

"Fine with me. Lucinda?"

"How about oatmeal frittatas, Lucinda?" said Falmouth. "Since I'm paying, and Matthew's driving."

It only took an accumulation of two ex-boyfriends acting uncharacteristically cheery to make a swarm, a blooming conspiracy. Lucinda wondered irritably whether she was missing a phone call at home. She wanted to tell Matthew and Falmouth how she was changed entirely, not who they took her to be, not a mere bassist or ex-girlfriend, foil for banter, kangaroo confidante. Her liaison and bender with the complainer had thrown her world off its rails, but not hers alone. If Matthew and Falmouth felt in some way changed this morning it was due to how the complainer had crept into their lives too, through the gallery telephones, through the lyrics and his secret collaboration with Bedwin. She wanted to tell them but the complainer's injunction of secrecy felt as profound as his touch, the trails he'd left across her.

Calls might be stacking up on her machine. If they spoke she'd want to see him. Anything seemed possible: Carl might even be waiting for her in her house, or outside it. The carousel only seemed stopped because she instead bumped along in Matthew's shockless Mazda, hell-bent for brunch. Matthew and Falmouth were at the moment discovering common ground, an animated cartoon they both liked, something to do with a Chihuahua and a cat. She should cherish this interlude, perhaps. Besides, she was ravenous for frittata. Sunlight strobed through the moonroof. She tilted her head back and shut her eyes to feel it batter her lids.


atthew explained to Falmouth about Fancher Autumnbreast's radio show, *The Dreaming Jaw*. Playing one of Autumnbreast's live in-studio sets had launched careers, everyone from the Rain Injuries to Souled American to Memorial Garage. Matthew also explained how Autumnbreast had been Janis Joplin's boyfriend, the only one, according to her, who'd never taken advantage of her. He'd also spent a famous weekend consoling Marianne Faithfull in Morocco after her breakup with Mick Jagger. The three of them sat outside, on Hugo's long deck, spectating as new brunchers grouped at tables around them. Their own chairs had been pushed back from the table, their meals demolished, oatmeal and egg white and curds scattered to plates' edges and beyond, juice glasses emptied, coffees filled a third and fourth time. Matthew's fingers stole across the settings to harvest appetizing chunks that had been abandoned on Falmouth's and Lucinda's plates. He looked healthier than in weeks, his sallowness fleshed again with glamour, with rock-star prospects. The kangaroo seemed forgotten for the moment.

Falmouth smoked and listened intently as Matthew talked, pursing his lips and shaking his head, stripped of irony. He interrogated Matthew precisely. It was as though his solipsism had been dissolved by the revelation of a rock-and-roll demimonde hiding in plain sight before him, now uncovered by the events of the Aparty.

"This person, this Autumnbreast, never wanted to play music himself?"

"He's more like the most virtuoso listener who ever lived," said Matthew. "When he listens, other people hear things. He's like a site, an occasion for things to happen. His radio show's like a clearing in the woods where the history of contemporary sound just happens to stroll through."

"See, I like that very much," said Falmouth. "It's not a passive role. His sensibility declares itself, and others pay attention. He's presiding."

"Right."

"Who cares?" said Lucinda.

They both stared.

"What a lot of malarkey. Presiding. You only like the way that sounds because it reminds you of yourself. It's like the gallery. You don't want to be an artist, it's too vulnerable. You want to be a collector instead, a curator of happenings. But that's what pushed you into the arms of Sniffles Harvey."

Falmouth blinked, smoked, refused to lash out.

"And you," she said, turning to Matthew. "You only like Autumnbreast because he calls you sweetheart, Matty-o, honey bunch."

"I don't think he actually called me honey bunch, Luce."

"I thought we were supposed to be an art band, something alternative." She felt herself growing vicious, couldn't quit. "I didn't realize you'd fall over your own feet getting caught up in some sleazy sixties rock dude's clutches."

"He's responsible for getting attention for a lot of alternative bands," said Matthew, with defensive precision.

"I've never heard of any of those bands you mentioned. Except the Rain Injuries. And you hate those guys."

"Well, that's probably because you don't listen to much of anything, Luce."

"Now, friends," said Falmouth, making an appeal for peace.

"And anyway, all those legendary women this clearing in the woods ever-so-sweetly presided over but never took advantage of," Lucinda continued, "I can't help noticing they were all conveniently smashed on alcohol or suffering a famously devastating breakup at the time."

"Huh?" said Matthew.

Lucinda's eyes stung. Her throat began to tighten and she understood, reluctantly, that she was crying. "I'm just saying Mr. Funbreast sounds like a rebound operator to me."

"What's the matter, Luce?" said Matthew.

"Nothing." She pressed her knuckles against her trembling chin, swallowed hard.

Falmouth stubbed his cigarette and peered at her. Lucinda fell silent, cast her gaze to the far avenue, shook the slime of tears from her cheeks.

"Did I say something?" said Matthew.

"We were only joking, Lucinda, whatever we said," said Falmouth.

"I'm fine."

"You're not fine, you're crying," said Falmouth.

"I'm fake-crying."

"Why would you do that?"

"For sympathy." She tucked what had welled, the joyous trauma of the past days, back into its hidden compartment. Something in Matthew might have been triggered by her sniping, however, or perhaps by the sight of her tears. He'd lapsed into his old recessive state, his joy in the gig unsustainable. Perhaps he'd also recalled Shelf the Flyer, maundering in her dismal basin.

"I wish I could fake cry as well as that," said Falmouth.

"I'll teach you."

"Sniffles Harvey—that was a good one."

"You don't even know how he earned that name."

"Of course I do. He was sniffling all around your band like a truffle pig. Trying to take credit for it himself, as if you were some strange lucky outgrowth of his loft."

"Let's give last night a break," said Lucinda. "Forget about Harvey and Summerbreast or any of these other spooky characters circling around."

"What other spooky characters?" said Falmouth.

"Nothing, I just mean let's give the whole thing a rest. Try to enjoy the morning."

"That's what we were doing," said Matthew.

"But not even mention the band, just pretend we're our regular selves."

"I think I just saw someone I think I know," said Falmouth, rising from his seat.

●

I t's like I got into some kind of horrible chess match with Dr. Marian. All I wanted was for them to take Shelf back into the general population. They said she was gouging the other kangaroos but solitary confinement is a self-perpetuating thing, she wasn't learning anything about proper socialization by being stuck in the pit." Matthew had begun to confess his and the kangaroo's dilemma the moment Falmouth had left him and Lucinda alone.

"They call it the pit?" asked Lucinda.

"Sure."

"That's what it looks like. I mean, that's what a visitor would probably call it. But there's something horrible about knowing that you people call it that too."

"It just kept escalating between us. I was totally discredited because I tried to go around Dr. Marian, to the board. Everyone in the office kept freezing me out."

"You appealed to the zoo's board about a single kangaroo?"

"I wrote a letter."

"Isn't Dr. Marian the one who hired you?"

"The bad vibes up at the office aren't really important anymore," he said. "My problem is I can't get anyone to pay attention now that I've, you know—taken Shelf away." Matthew sagged in his chair as though only now relieved of some burden of denial, as if Lucinda and Denise hadn't broken in and seen for themselves. Perhaps he'd persuaded himself that episode was truly a dream, a kangaroo piss-fever hallucination.

"You want attention for that?"

"My plan was to leak it and embarrass the zoo. I tried to get the *Times* and the *Weekly* to come and see Shelf. I said I was holding her hostage to protest her treatment. I even tried News Eleven. But they won't return my calls."

"I don't understand."

"Dr. Marian outflanked me. When the paper or the television calls, she says the zoo's not missing any kangaroos. They think I'm a crank. She won't even confirm that I worked there, just says I'm familiar to them, a publicity hound, some kind of zoological stalker, and that attention only encourages me. At the same time, she won't admit to anyone at the zoo that I'm fired. Actually, I'm not fired."

"What?"

"The department secretary called and said they were holding my paychecks in the office, but they won't forward them. They're trying to get me to come in, so they can surround me and conduct some kind of brainwashing."

"That sounds a little paranoid."

"You get used to putting a gorilla in a straitjacket or shooting an ibex in the throat with a twelve-ounce dart you'd be surprised what you'd be willing to do to a human being, Luce. These people are like Nazi doctors, they've persuaded themselves they're engaged with primal factors outside the ken of normal human beings."

"Were you ever recruited to join some kind of vigilante faction? I suppose the gorillas themselves could be employed in death squads, after enough shock treatment."

"Don't make fun of me." He shrank into the corner of his

chair, his eyes revealing real fear, as if the restaurant might be surrounded at that moment by Dr. Marian's operatives.

"It can't be easy, just the two of you in that apartment," Lucinda said, gently now, thinking of that dungeon of lettuce and urine.

"I've been telling myself it's going to get better," Matthew droned, ponderous in his guilt.

"You probably thought it would be different when you got her out of the pit."

"I think she blames me. I used to be the one who cheered her up. We'd talk and she'd lift her head and I could tell she didn't want me to leave. Now it's like she associates me with the zoo. She won't even look at me."

"Moving in together might not have been the best idea."

"She has a problem with high expectations," Matthew said, his gaze on some middle distance, as if facing some unseen advocate for the kangaroo, a mediator or marriage counselor. "It began with her parents."

"What about her parents?"

"Shelf was born right here, in Los Angeles. Her parents were sort of famous. They were sent here as a gift to Linda Ronstadt from an Australian fan. Linda Ronstadt didn't know what to do with them, so she gave them to the zoo. There was a lot of publicity at the time, and I think it was confusing for the kangaroos. They got special treatment and then were expected to melt into the regular population. I suppose they imparted a certain lack of realistic perspective to Shelf."

"Maybe Fancher Autumnbreast should take her to Morocco," said Lucinda. "It worked for Marianne Faithfull."

"Either you want to help me or you don't, Lucinda."

"I'm sorry. Tell me what I can do. I'm hardly a kangaroo person."

"Go and collect my checks," he said. "I'm totally broke."

"They'd let me?"

"It's worth a try. At least there's nothing they can do to you."

Lucinda reached across the table and nudged Matthew's fingertips, offered a smile. An immense noontime melancholy had suffused their table. The lives at nearby tables, pairs of couples, families, the clank of silver and happy conversation, all evoked what they'd deserted. Their days were rich and strange, full of kangaroos and gigs, things other brunchers couldn't know, but they were impoverished too, bereft of ordinary solidarities which had once seemed near at hand as the spoons and forks on the table between them, as their browsing fingertips.

The fugue dissolved and they noticed Falmouth. He sat at another table, deep in the porch's shadow, legs crossed, scribbling on a pad propped across his knee. As they turned to him he lifted his pen from the page and squinted at the results.

"What's that?" said Lucinda.

"I'm entering a new phase of radical openness to suggestion. It took you and Jules Harvey to make me understand. You've been taking an admirable risk with your horrible music. From this point on my only conceptual medium will be myself. My own behavior and choices, the way I respond to the opportunities to transform daily experience into art. I'm done trying to bully others into being my canvas and oils, in other words."

"That's nice, but what are you doing?"

"I borrowed this pen and pad from the waitress," he said. "She's one of my students. It's only ballpoint and it skips but I think that's good, a happy accident, the kind of thing I'll be open to from now on."

"Okay, but what are you drawing?"

"You."

He turned the pad around. Matthew and Lucinda were depicted in feathery blue ballpoint strokes, seated with their heads leaned together at the table, under shelter of the deck. Another figure loomed between them, paws bridging their shoulders, pointy ears brushing the porch, feet crammed under their table. Long whiskers extended from the grinning cartoon mammal's nose, past Lucinda's and Matthew's heads, radiating like beams of light in a child's drawing of the sun.

"Is that a ten-foot rat?" said Lucinda. "Or your idea of a kangaroo?"

Falmouth shrugged. "It's me, really. A spirit-representation of my love and concern for you on this beautiful morning."

"You're a strange person, Falmouth."

"Thank you."

"Were you listening to us talk?"

"Half listening."

"So, any half thoughts?"

"On what?" Falmouth reversed his pad and resumed sketching, squinting at them like some alfresco painter. The morning had drifted to afternoon, a sweet languor investing in their bodies and words. Cars swooped on the 101, a long block away, but the sitters on Hugo's porch went contentedly nowhere, weekending.

"You're a master of provocation, Falmouth. What about taking on the Los Angeles Zoo?"

"I've never been one for causes."

Matthew had eased into silence, disburdened of his secrets and fears. Anyone could speak of zoos and kangaroos now. These were public facts, not some private concern.

"Think of it as a performance piece," said Lucinda.

"I'm out of that line, I told you. Sounds more like a job for Sniffles Harvey."

"Screw Harvey. If you help with the zoo we'd let you manage our band. Like Andy Warhol and the Velvet Underground." Lucinda pictured him as the giant mammal, his tender ghostly paws on their shoulders, guiding the band forward.

"I don't want to manage anything, thank you." Examining his work, Falmouth ran fingers spotty with ink over his sweaty dome and left a blue smudge high on his brow. He shrugged conclusively and tore the page from the waitress's pad. "Here. I award you the first result, a token of my affection."

"Thank you," said Lucinda.

"It's great," said Matthew, barely looking.

"Are you hungry again?" said Falmouth. "I know it's ridiculous, but I could eat."

"I'm starved," said Matthew inattentively. He stretched his legs under the table, his posture oblique and catlike. He'd shifted back into his body, recovered his vanity.

"Let's go to San Pedro and get crabs," said Lucinda. "It seems like nobody ever goes to San Pedro anymore."

"That's a long way," said Falmouth.

"You wouldn't say that if you'd had these crabs. Also the Mexican garlic bread they've got on the wharf. When's the last time you saw the Pacific Ocean, Falmouth?"

"Oh, I've seen the ocean. It's you pale starving musicians who never go west of La Cienega."

"And the beer," said Lucinda. "The beer tastes good by the water."

"I'd have to get gas," mused Matthew.

"Do they have bibs?" said Falmouth, glancing at his spotless white shirt. He flagged the waitress, motioning with her own pen for the check. They'd go to San Pedro, it was unmistakable, but there was pleasure in protracting the debate, letting their craving grow. Hugo's kitchen was still pumping out frittatas heaped with curds for late brunchers, while sparrows crept at their feet pilfering crumbs and the indolent hours unfurled. Maybe elsewhere Lucinda's phone rang off the hook. Maybe a disgruntled Shelf shredded Matthew's shower curtain or was pillaging his kitchen, maybe Falmouth's gallery had been set on fire by irate complainers, it didn't matter. Today, the day after the Aparty, they were escape artists, had dissolved their grievances in the coffee and sunlight, and now nothing could touch them. They'd become that rarest version of themselves, uncomplainers.

h e did not call. He had not called. There was no call. Not, anyway, on Saturday. By the time Matthew dropped Lucinda at her doorstep it was nearly dark again and, happily polluted with beer and lemon butter–drenched crabs and just one margarita, fingernails still grainy with pepper and salt, she'd not troubled to think of Carl, her complainer, for hours, since the moment on Hugo's deck when, long having decided not to speak of him to Falmouth or Matthew she'd also realized she could free herself of any thought of him, for at least the day. If she were in love with him he'd return to her mind, just as if he were in love with her he'd surely ring her phone. Not that it meant the opposite if he hadn't. He never had, she realized, never at that number, only on the complaint line. Not that she'd rushed home to check. Blotted with beer and sunshine, she'd thought of anything else, or nothing, at her doorstep. Instead embraced her friend-exes, each of whom had stepped from the car to make farewells. Or perhaps Falmouth only moved from the backseat to the passenger seat she'd vacated. Anyway, they embraced. She kissed them both with tongue, for sport. Falmouth, then Matthew. Both met her with surprised but willing mouths, as if caught forming a word to remain unspoken. They tasted of garlic and beer. Falmouth of cigarettes too. If neither utterly swooned to her kiss neither rebuffed her. Besides, she gave them barely a chance. Just tongue and a smudge of her hips and goodbye. She checked the machine with her keys still in her hand, the light switch unreached, not so much thinking of the complainer in particular, just drunken automatism. He hadn't called. He didn't call Sunday, either.

# four

he receptionist wore a lab coat and black-frame glasses, and perhaps wasn't a receptionist at all but a zoological veterinarian who'd taken a seat at the receptionist's desk. She was too young, though, to be Dr. Marian. The girl sat alone paging through the newspaper and eating a drippy egg-salad sandwich and Lucinda had to speak to get her attention, feeling more like an intruder than she'd expected, Matthew's paranoia rubbed off on her. She was within her public citizen's rights to stroll into the zoo's offices, she reminded herself.

"Excuse me for bothering you. I, ah, need to pick up some checks."

"Checks?"

"For, um—" Lucinda mimed questing for a name on her tongue's tip, then glanced at a scrap of paper yanked from her pocket: "Matthew, yes, Matthew Plangent."

"I think he's sick."

"Sorry?"

"He's out sick."

"Oh, right, that's why I'm picking up his—materials."

"What kind of materials?"

"Paychecks and any other materials that would be waiting here for him."

The girl shrugged and tipped her chin in the direction of a grid of twenty or thirty cubbyholes on the wall at Lucinda's left. These were labeled with last names, alphabetically. Lucinda scooped the bundle of envelopes and circulars that filled Matthew's cubby and tucked them into her bag, trusting the checks to be among them.

"Is there a Dr. Marian or someone with that name here?"

"Down the hall to your right."

The brass nameplate beside the pebbled-glass door read MARIAN RORSCHACH, B.V.SC., M.R.C.V.S., PH.D., DIRECTOR. The door was ajar, but Lucinda paused to rap on the glass. Classical music seeped from the room.

"Yes?"

"Dr. Marian?" Lucinda parsed a silhouette moving against a daylit window, fragmented to pixels by the door's glass. She felt her heart lurch, regretting her gambit at the last moment, too late.

"Come in."

Marian Rorschach wore a white coat too, over a black turtleneck that reminded Lucinda of Matthew's own frequent costume, though Dr. Rorschach's had been stretched around gallon-size breasts where Matthew's was draped on a skeleton. Her heavy-fleshed face was deeply handsome, dark eyes glittering in pouchy seats. Her full black hair, bound Japanese-style in a sagging bun, bore a skunklike streak of white. She gnawed a paper clip while she studied a sheaf of papers open on her computerless desk as Lucinda entered. Now she removed the clip from the corner of her mouth and twisted a dial on a small transistor radio at her desk's corner, lowering the volume.

"Can I help you?"

"I'd like to speak with you for a moment."

"Concerning?"

"I write for the *Echo Park Annoyance*," said Lucinda. "I'm here concerning an alleged marsupial that may have been expropriated from your premises."

"Expropriated."

"In so many words, yes."

Dr. Marian raised one eyebrow and gestured at a leather chair to one side of the desk. "Sit down."

"Thank you, I'll stand." The chair was low and soft, a possible bid for advantage on the part of Dr. Marian.

"What's your name?"

"My name isn't important."

"I see, I see." Dr. Marian tapped her pen against her desk and studied Lucinda. "You talk like a cop," she said suddenly, her tone heavy.

"Thank you," blurted Lucinda.

"But I don't think that's where you got this wrong impression of yours," Dr. Marian continued. "In fact, I don't think you really know anything about any alleged marsupials at all, not from the sound of things."

"You might think that and be wrong," said Lucinda. This sport of insinuation recalled a game she'd played as a child, of pulling her fingers from underneath another child's hands and slapping them on top, an escapade which inevitably turned frantic, then painful. "For all you know this rookie reporter might have stumbled into a very close encounter with the alleged aforementioned."

"I'm glad you say rookie," said Dr. Marian. "It saves me saying it."

"I meant eager and tireless, not gullible."

"Gullible is another excellent word I thank you for supplying."

Lucinda opted for bluntness. "Your establishment is missing a kangaroo, sir."

"Don't call me sir. We're missing nothing."

"One of your protégés has gone guerrilla."

"The person in question is a malingerer who takes too many sick days, nothing more."

Lucinda found herself trembling under Dr. Marian's imperious command. She understood Matthew better now, seeing the regime he'd been negotiating. It aroused her sympathy, and a kind of jealousy as well.

"The person in question liberated a martyr kangaroo," said Lucinda, working to keep any sulkiness from her voice.

"A foolish legend that I've heard circulating."

"I've seen the captive, living anonymously among apartment dwellers, like Patty Hearst."

"As I told the police, no sane person, let alone a zoo employee, would keep a kangaroo in an urban apartment. For one thing an adult kangaroo defecates three or four times a day with results approximately the size of a baseball glove, a catcher's mitt specifically."

"No sane person," Lucinda echoed.

"That's what I said."

"There's sense in that." Lucinda felt herself bent helplessly, like light in a prism, into service to Dr. Marian's interests.

"I'm glad you see the sense in what I say."

"Of course certain persons might in certain local situations have acted less sane than other certain persons might have hoped. And would now therefore be facing more or less exactly a three-to-four-catcher's-mitts-per-day type of situation."

"There's only one answer for a person in that type of situation," said Dr. Marian. Lucinda noticed, perhaps too late, a susceptibility in Dr. Marian's responses for matching her interrogator's rhythms. Might this have been exploited? More likely it was only a glimpse of Dr. Marian's ability to absorb and redirect what came within her orbit, particularly anything threatening to the zoo's priorities.

"What's the answer?" said Lucinda.

"Get sane in a hurry."

"I see. And if that person were to want to come in from the cold, so to speak?"

"As you should understand from what I've said, it is and always will be a nonevent."

"Thank you."

"My pleasure." Dr. Marian gestured at the door. Lucinda found herself moving toward it.

"Dr. Marian?"

"Yes?"

"You haven't ever given any thoughts to lending your gifts to a greater variety of causes, say for instance to managing a very promising rock-and-roll band?"

"Is that a question you ask at the end of every interview?"

"Sorry?"

"I don't read the *Annoyance*, and I was wondering whether that was some sort of generic question, like what is your favorite color or are you a morning person or a night person, or if it had something to do with my work at the zoo."

"No, it isn't generic. You're an extraordinary negotiator and I just wondered if you would ever think of representing a musician or group."

"I'd have to hear their music first."

"Thank you very much," said Lucinda. "I won't take any more of your time."

a carpenter pried with his hammer's claw at the joints of the cubicle, squeaking a bent nail from agonized plywood. Beside him Lucinda sat in the middle of the gallery floor with an unringing telephone between her knees. The complaint office was being hurriedly disassembled, subject to Falmouth's hostility to lazy transitions. Lucinda and the interns had convened to handle a last round of calls, while Falmouth himself tore the black paper from the storefront windows. The phrase "no more complaints," with which he'd instructed them to answer the phones, had already cued sobbing panic in a few habitual callers.

The cubicle dividers fell and bands of afternoon light saturated the deeper recesses of the gallery. The interns appeared exhilarated by the destruction. In intervals between murmured farewells to their complainers they refreshed themselves with yoga postures and cigarettes, with takeout Chinese and flirting with the carpenters. Falmouth fretted among them, sidestepping whisk-broomed piles of chips and dust that might accrue to his black cuffs. After the weekend's dissolution he'd donned a crisp suit, scraped head and chin free of stubble. His firm gaze didn't confess any memory of a crab-salty kiss. Lucinda sat alone taking sporadic calls, pining for what she hadn't known she'd miss. The only complainer who mattered hadn't called. Now the stage set was being struck.

By evening the carpenters were gone. Falmouth's interns wandered like cats in the lengthening shadows, cradling their phones. But by seven the calls had begun to trail away. The interns yawned, asked to be excused, delivered a round of hugs, vanished. Falmouth rinsed their chopsticks and he and Lucinda set into the cold ruin of takeout, prawns and snow peas sunk in an aspic of cornstarch and vinegar.

"I guess I need a job," said Lucinda.

"Or a number-one record."

"I need to pay the rent in two weeks. I may have to go back to the factory where they assemble cappuccinos."

"Stay on the payroll. You can write my grant proposals."

"What are you doing next?"

"Our official line will be nothing."

A neatly zipped black leather portfolio leaned against Falmouth's desk. He bore as well a telltale smudge of graphite on the heel of his right hand. Crumbs of pink eraser decorated his lap. He'd been drawing again. She didn't confront him.

"Why can't you say you're doing nothing yourself?" she said.

"It's better if I pay you to say it."

They pushed the meal into the garbage. Falmouth moved to the master panel to switch off the overhead lights, but Lucinda said, "I think I'll stay a bit longer."

Falmouth raised his eyebrows.

"They'll start ringing again around nine," she said. "They always do."

"I was afraid someone would get sentimental," he said. "I didn't realize it would be you. I asked the phone company to cancel the number. It should be cut off shortly after midnight."

He left her alone there. The institute was an ember flaring on the brink of ash. Falmouth was right. Lucinda stayed for more than just the hope of the complainer's call. She was a secret curator now. When they rang she answered in the old way. Let them think nothing had changed, until it was too late. She was Florence Nightingale, or a nun among the lepers. A man told her he'd suffered a paper cut on his testicle. Another said his nephew had stolen his collection of vintage lobby cards. A woman or possibly a child made a sound like a rabbit gnawing a carrot.

She thought about dialing the complainer's number and didn't.

The sixth or seventh caller was Denise. "There you are," said the drummer. "Let's go out."

"I'm sort of on a vigil. A person might phone me here."

"The one from the other night?"

"Yes." They both knew who they were talking about. "Maybe you could come here."

"You want something to drink?"

"Maybe pick up a six."

"A six it is."

"And hey, Denise?"

"Yes?"

"Who cut your hair?"

"I did it myself."

"A six and scissors."

h e walked into the storefront, an hour after Denise. They'd forgotten to lock the door, and sat deep in the gallery's rear, ignoring the line's sporadic ringing. Lucinda sat encircled by her former hair, which lay in a pattern suggesting a controlled explosion. She'd removed her shoes and shirt, wore above her jeans only a pale blue brassiere, its surface furred with a hectic chiaroscuro of hair, as were her neck and shoulders and the knees of her jeans. Denise maypoled around Lucinda in her chair, a bottle in one hand, shears in the other, squinting and burping, making hedging adjustments to her initial ferocious attack. They had no mirror.

The complainer appeared in their ring of light and Lucinda's hands flew up to feel the spiky new contours of her head. There was an obscure shame in his seeing the haircut sooner than her. A trickling of hair rained from her lifted arms into the hoisted cleft of her breasts, making her feel even more unhidden. Not that there was any privilege he hadn't already claimed, or she hadn't offered gladly. He smiled and scratched his jaw and she was struck again by the slightly penisy glamour of his cleft chin and nose, his sculpted lips, his baggy eyes. His hand slid to his stomach, to stuff his flopped shirttails into his belt, as though unconsciously feeling he ought to make some effort, having intruded on a scene of grooming.

"You're the drummer," he said.

"Denise."

"Carl. Nice to meet you."

"You were at the show."

"Oh, yes," he said shyly. "It was sensational."

"Thank you."

"Want a beer?" said Lucinda.

"Sure, thanks."

Lucinda handed a bottle to the complainer from the six beneath her chair, then twisted the cap off a fresh one for herself. Clipped ends floated as she moved, as though she dwelled in a snow globe of hair.

Denise found a push broom and plowed clippings into an ersatz animal behind Lucinda's chair. Lucinda darted up and brushed herself against the complainer, parted lips raking his collar, then turned, huddling in her goose-pimpled arms, to fetch her shirt.

"Don't stop on my account," said the complainer, taking a long pull on his beer. "I'll just sit and watch."

"It doesn't look finished?" Lucinda slid her T-shirt and sweater, still balled together, over her head, scattering more hair.

"I'm no judge. It seems you're after a hairstyle that complements the band's sound, something wild and natural, like a flock of hedgehogs. Are you going to confront the singer, though? Because now he's the only one with girlish hair."

"Matthew."

"And the person on the stool is Bedwin, is that right?"

"Yes."

"I'll play keyboards, I guess."

Lucinda put her finger to her lips, though she felt a thrill at the image, Carl's big shoulders hunched over a Farfisa organ, jostling onstage somewhere between Bedwin's stool and Denise's kit.

"I feel like you're Lucinda's imaginary friend," said Denise, not seeming to have noticed his remark. "Like I'm not really supposed to be able to see you."

Lucinda widened her eyes at Carl: I haven't told our secret, she beamed into his thoughts. He couldn't reasonably be angry that Denise had noticed their embrace at Jules Harvey's loft. Lucinda realized she wanted Denise to know.

The complainer seemed not to register Lucinda's alarm. He drew a chair from the gallery's darkened corner, into their pool of light, and seated himself. "I'd make some joke about how difficult it is for us imaginary friends," he said. "The constant struggle to remain visible, etcetera. But the truth is I think it's you guys, the band, I mean, who are figments of *my* imagination."

Lucinda vibrated, hearing his voice, seeing him here again before her, real. Since the night of the gig and their parting she'd binged on drink and crabs, talked on telephones and operated heavy machinery, even sort of kissed someone else, two someone elses. Swimming in her desultory bedsheets Sunday morning she'd masturbated three times, the last humping the ridge of a throw pillow. Yet it all seemed less than a parenthesis now, events not even so vivid as dreams, more like tableaux glimpsed on a television playing in the background somewhere, one no one had thought to switch off.

"How are we figments of your imagination?" said Denise. She inspected him defiantly, wary of sarcasm. She'd pulled up a rolling office chair and plopped down, stretching her legs between Carl and Lucinda as if to assert that she wouldn't be reduced to third-wheel status.

The complainer emptied his beer with a satisfied gasp, put the bottle aside. "Just a minute," he said, and drew a matchbox from his shirt pocket. He slid open its drawer to produce a tightly rolled joint, then struck a match to spark its tip. "Here's the thing," he said, through his first whalelike indraft and burst of exhaled fume. "I spent the last few days thinking about this. It really knocked me for a loop at first. You singing my songs, I mean."

"Your songs?" said Denise. Lucinda was struck dumb, could only listen.

"My little scribblings, my first drafts," he said. He handed the joint to Lucinda. "My complaints, whatever you want to call them. That was you scratching away with a pen on the other end of the line, wasn't it?"

Lucinda nodded, hypnotized. Carl was claiming the band. She couldn't justifiably object. Any ground she stood on was under water, tide lapping at her knees or higher. In truth, she wanted him to have what he liked. That was in the nature of her discovery, her strange new love. More, the aura of her submission widened to enclose Denise as well. Lucinda was only curious about what the complainer might make Denise do.

Lucinda drew weakly on the joint, crossing her eyes to be certain its lit end flared. She'd never been a cigarette smoker, and when she puffed marijuana she felt like a fraud, contriving at an act natural to others. Clutching at a lungful, she passed the smoldering joint to Denise, as if to transmit some whiff of complicity. Denise accepted it without meeting Lucinda's eye.

"The things you said, the things that became lyrics, you were thinking them for the first time when you said them to me, right?" Lucinda heard plaintiveness leak into her voice.

Carl shrugged. "Hard to say. I'm always worrying away at one motif or another. I was taken with what you did with 'monster eyes' and 'astronaut food.'"

"Everyone likes 'Monster Eyes,'" Lucinda gushed, grateful to escape to this point of universal consent.

"It's got itchiness, like I was telling you," said the complainer. "Everyone likes it because everyone thinks it's about them. Like a decal of the soul. I'd say I wish I'd thought it up myself, if I hadn't."

"You thought up 'Monster Eyes'?" said Denise. She sucked at the joint, gobbling smoke like a pro, even as she squinted at Carlton in suspicion.

"The words came out of this mouth."

"You didn't mean them as a song, though," urged Lucinda.

"No, I imagined I was seducing you," he admitted. "Which I seem to have done while writing a song in my spare time. I'm very impressed with myself."

Denise's gaze was fixed on Carlton, as if to meet his challenge with the most essential part of herself, more on the band's behalf than on Lucinda's. She kept the marijuana cigarette tucked between her fingers, her cupped hand hovering near her mouth, puffing very slightly. Lucinda had seen before how the drummer would enter a state of fierce intoxication, crafting a thick foggy lens of drug or drink through which to peer out at the world, a transparent shield. "So you tricked Lucinda into using your shitty lyrics," she said. Her tone wasn't wholly unfriendly. "And now you want to take credit for songs that were basically written by Bedwin, someone you've never met."

"I'd like very much to meet him."

"Do you want to destroy the band?"

"How could I want to do that?" he said. "I basically am the band."

"What do you want out of this? What exactly do you think is going to happen?"

"I want what we all want," said Carl. "To move certain parts of the interior of myself into the external world, to see if they can be embraced. What's incredible is that it happened without my knowledge. Like putting on clothes somebody laid out on a bed for you and finding the pockets are full of money and car keys and an address book full of new friends."

"Now you're getting to the point," said Denise. "You see us as a fund of young new friends." She handed the joint back to him, reduced to a mushy nub. "One of whom you get to fuck."

"Isn't there a tradition of liaisons within musical groups?" he said. "I'm surprised you don't have any already."

"I can choose who I fuck, Denise," said Lucinda.

"I didn't mean to suggest it wasn't your choice. Though if I were in the mood for white hair I'd be more inclined to go for that Fancher Autumnbreast, myself. At least he's sort of a hipster. No offense, Carl, but you don't really look like a member of a rock-and-roll band."

"None taken. Maybe I should ask you for a haircut."

"I wouldn't fool with that," said Denise. "Your long hair is all you've got going for you. We could dye it black or orange, maybe. But then we'd have to do your eyebrows, too. It's probably hopeless."

"I can dress up like this Autumnbreast, if you tell me how. I've never seen him, just heard his voice on the radio."

"It's not the clothes but how you wear them."

"I'm sure that's true. Like our singer, Matthew. Is that who you're drawn to, personally?"

"You don't know me well enough to ask me that, Carl," said Denise. She might have turned a little red.

"You're right, it's better for band members to leave these things unspoken," said Carl.

"I didn't say anything like that."

"Maybe I misread the onstage vibes."

"Being in a band isn't about hair or clothes," said Lucinda, wanting to blunt the hostilities. "The point is the music." The assertion, which she'd only uttered as a diversion, seemed instantly both profound and obvious. She waited for Carl's and Denise's acclaim, not so much to confirm her point as to test their grasp of essential realities.

"That may be true," said Carl. He siphoned the soggy nubbin of joint, then tossed it sideways into the shadows of the gallery. "Only, as a good friend of mine used to say, you can't be deep without a surface."

They stared at him, the bass player and drummer, trying to digest the phrase, which conveyed itself into their minds like a drug itself: toxic, gnarled, ineradicable.

"Deep without a surface," repeated Denise.

"Yes," said Carlton. "You can't be, that's the point."

"That's the stupidest thing I've ever heard."

Lucinda understood that Denise only meant it as a brave show of resistance to the phrase's colonizing effects.

"Did a good friend of yours really used to say that?" said Lucinda. She felt obscurely jealous.

"No, I made it up just now."

"That could be the name of an album," said Denise. *"Deep Without a Surface."*

"The kind of guys who name an album that would have songs that each took up a whole side," said Lucinda.

"They could be called the Deep Surfaces," said Denise.

"Or Deep and the Surfaces," said Lucinda. "There wouldn't be any pictures of them on the record sleeve."

"Just their instruments," said Denise. "Because all that matters is the music."

"Whereas for our band the opposite is true," said the complainer.

Again they stared at him as if his words had opened up some pit in the floor.

"I just realized," said Denise. " 'You can't be deep without a surface' describes the situation perfectly. The lyrics you wrote, they wouldn't amount to anything at all if we hadn't played them onstage. They wouldn't be worth ten cents if they weren't coming out of Matthew's mouth."

"Matthew makes a very nice human bumper sticker or coffee mug," said Carl.

"If you tried to take his place it wouldn't work," said Denise.

"I'm not taking his place, I'm assuming my own."

"You act like you're some skinny backup singer, some inconspicuous element. We're not an orchestra, Carl. We can't just give you a tambourine and hide you behind an amp or something."

"A lot of groups have five members, don't they?"

"Have you looked in the mirror? Remember when they tried to put Frankenstein in a tuxedo? What was that movie?"

*"Last Tango in Paris?"*

"Exactly."

Lucinda felt vertigo watching Carl and Denise's jesting struggle. She wished to brush away their banter, wave it off like smoke. Was the complainer moving nearer to Lucinda, or farther away? It seemed both at once. She wanted him to want her body, not her band. She wished to be swallowed, laid open with her robe undone across a dirty yellow chair. But his appetite seemed to be drifting. There was confusion here too, since the image of the dirty yellow chair came from a song, though not originally. That was the problem: Carlton's claim on the band was perversely justified, and impossible to disentangle. The more Denise denied him that claim the further he inched in, an intrusion that would have seemed impossible an hour earlier.

"Nobody takes Matthew seriously," said Lucinda. "Last week at the supermarket I saw a woman watching him like he was an ocelot on a nature show, like she wanted to go to the pet store and buy one for herself. It's not so easy being a human bumper sticker."

"Sad," said Carl.

"It is sad. The whole band relies on his charisma. We're exploiting him. I think he senses it."

"There's nothing sadder than being a genius of sex," said the complainer. "Evoking nothing but pleasure in the eyes of others."

"I never thought of it that way," said Denise. "It's sort of an involuntary condition."

"In another age people like him became priests or nuns," said Lucinda dreamily.

"Let's go out and beat up some unattractive people," said Carl.

Lucinda and Denise stared at him. He raised his hands as

if at gunpoint. "Though arguably that would be taking things too far."

Denise sprang from her chair, fitful. "Matthew's not the problem," she said. She seemed to be carrying on some internal dialogue. "Matthew can take care of himself." She began to pace, stalking the perimeter of their chairs like the zoo's coyote working its cage's limits. "I'm thinking of Bedwin now."

"Bedwin?"

"Yes, he'd have to be treated gently. The band is his whole planet, he doesn't know anything else."

Carl shrugged. "So his planet just got a little more—various."

"You don't know him," said Lucinda. "All he does is watch the same black-and-white movie over and over and write songs."

"He could take the fact that he collaborated unknowingly with someone like you very badly," said Denise. She hung on the rim of darkness, her features shrouded, as though playing to an unseen crowd. Her words seemed to take it for granted that the three of them all dwelled within some common understanding or intention.

"Who does he think wrote the lyrics?" said Carl.

"If I understand Bedwin, he doesn't think about it. He might not even remember which ones are his and which Lucinda brought to him."

"Sounds fine to me," said Carlton. "Why not just leave it at that?"

"What do you mean?"

"When somebody's living in a delusory world, it isn't necessarily your job to pull them out of it. Not unless you've got a better one to offer in its place."

"You mean a better delusion?" said Lucinda.

Carl shrugged, as if to say, *What else?* "What needs saying? Doesn't he trust the two of you?"

"Of course."

"So what do you say we just leave it up to us?"

Denise strolled the shadow boundary, no longer agitated. She glanced at Lucinda, perhaps seeking a sign. Lucinda and the complainer sat in a triangle with Denise's vacated chair, under lights still wreathed in smoke. Lucinda had abandoned her sneakers on the floor and raised her socked feet to the chair's lip, hugging her knees to her breasts. Carlton sprawled in the abdicated space between them, his thighs spread wide, one foot upright and the other limply horizontal, between Lucinda's empty sneakers, his posture grotesquely unashamed and inviting. His shirt was misbuttoned, skewed, riding up to expose a river of hair. Carl was pubic all the way to his neck.

The complainer had plopped himself in the middle of her life and band. Perhaps it was Falmouth's fault. Carl had found his way to her ear, like a hummingbird pollinating a flower, solely due to Falmouth's foolish project. The interns had planted stickers and had drawn the attention of an author of stickers, like calling to like, a coyote's howl across canyons. Perhaps Carlton's entry into the band should be seen in this light, as Falmouth's latest art piece, committed unconsciously. Lucinda felt a clandestine devotion to Falmouth, whose imagination embraced more than he knew. But Falmouth was in her past, as was Matthew. Beautiful fallen displaced Matthew.

She could choose who to fuck. Her own words. And she had. She felt her choice in a place in her throat, a hollow pressurized walnut she couldn't gulp away. She knew it at the juncture where her crossed heels sought the seam of her jeans, where she'd begun to sway and mash against herself, to covertly masturbate, just a little. The room seemed to tilt, to urge her forward in her chair. She stared at Carl. Carlton Complainer. To choose who to fuck is to choose who gets to fuck you. But not how. That was for them to know and you to find out. Lucinda was ready for Denise to leave now. She uncoiled from her chair and moved across to slide into Carl's lap, made herself small enough to occupy him like a landscape. He grasped her hip and cinched her nearer to him. Kissed her hair, as she squirreled at his neck. A long moment elapsed, one that might have been five or twenty minutes. She sensed dimly Denise waving a silent goodbye, somewhere out of the range where anything much mattered. Then heard a click as the distant gallery door was shut against an instant's susurrus of wheels tracing Sunset's blacktop.

"I want a drink," she said, even as she struggled at the buttons of his fly, trying to free him from his jeans.

"Let's get you one."

"I don't even know your last name," she said.

"Vogelsong."

"No," she said.

"No?"

"I don't like it. It doesn't sound like you." With the native urgency of a child squatting to urinate on a highway shoulder she bunched her pants and underwear at her thighs, then lowered herself like a mouth. He hardened within her. She grunted, shuddering high in her gullet, lengthening her back, arraying herself like a question mark above him, a long doubting curl culminating in one irrefutable point.

"I can't help it," he sighed. "It's my name."

"Vocalsong, what's that, it's like Wetwater or Flavortaste or something—"

"It's German," he said. "Vogel means bird." The complainer's nostrils widened, the only evidence he was more than a venue for Lucinda's tremors.

"Birdsong?"

"Song isn't song. It comes from Vogelfang. It means fowling."

It was a while before she could produce her question. "Fowling?"

"Catching fowls."

"You mean hunting," she said. "Catching their hearts with bullets."

"I guess that's right."

"Carlton Birdkiller." She slid from him now, between his legs, to the floor. She'd orgasmed, he hadn't.

"Carl," he corrected.

"Carl Birdkiller."

He rebuttoned himself. "You want to get a drink?"

"Yes, please."

# five

the band shed their instruments in their accustomed places, scattered across the vast Persian carpet at the west-facing windows of Carl Vogelsong's thirtieth-story Olive Street condominium, a loft as high-placed above its surroundings as Jules Harvey's, though otherwise its opposite. Harvey dwelled in a spartan corner, leaving the rest of his space as a tabula rasa for the enactment of public schemes, whereas the complainer spread his living space to every corner, saturating the cavernous room with antique furniture, lead-glass floor lamps and glass-paneled bookshelves, local arrangements of love seats and divans suggesting rooms without walls. His bed was partitioned from the wider space by a floor-brushing green velvet curtain on a polished wooden rail, and his lavish kitchen was formed of an archipelago of countertops and appliances around a monolithic six-burner range, a kind of theater-in-the-round in the loft's middle. The complainer had hired a moving van and crew to shift the band's equipment into the loft, having first cleared the blood-and-rust-colored carpet, itself the size of Denise's whole living room, as a practice space.

In the past weeks the band had clocked their rehearsals to the sunset's glow, as if claiming the power to orchestrate the melting of the continent's last light into the far-twinkling surf. Then, usually, the complainer would order in Vietnamese or Sushi takeout, lemongrass chicken or Ventura hand rolls. The band would unpack white folded paper boxes across his oak table, a four-leaf large enough to bear piles of books and scatterings of ashtrays full of joint butts and a corral of the previous night's wine-stained glasses at one end and still invitingly seat five or six at the other. Tonight, however, the table had been cleared, a starched cloth thrown over it, the complainer's best china and crystal set out. While they practiced, Falmouth had been cooking, boiling down onions and garlic and pork sausages in a tremendous black skillet, brewing what he called his legendary sauce.

Falmouth had become domesticated to the band. Summer break had freed him from his teaching. With no students to impress he'd slacked in both conceptual edge and dress code, though his white T-shirts were uniformly crisp and bright, as if pulled from a dispenser like tissues. Since the disbanding of the complaint center his gallery remained barren. He'd done nothing but scribble in enormous spiral-bound pads with crayon or ballpoint, whatever lay at hand. A fly-on-the-wall at rehearsals, he'd by now produced dozens of sketches of the five working at their music, a pile of pages he shucked from his book as they were done, offering them to the band or letting them fall at his feet. Someone—Bedwin? Denise?—had draped the discarded pages in a stack on the glass top of one of the complainer's several pinball machines, where they formed a loose dossier of the band's incorporation of Carl and his small, upright organ into their company.

Carlton stood, as in Lucinda's vision, between Bedwin, who still played seated, now in a salvaged barber's chair, and Denise's drums. He and Lucinda shared a mike stand. The band had slackened, made room, inching to the edges of the Persian. The complainer's noodly organ riffs and atonal backing vocals found a place too, in a middle of their sound the band might not otherwise have known existed. Like a checker cab with an extra seat, they could carry him. When they played "Monster Eyes," the song that was their signature, their credential, Carl shouted his backing vocals, and played his wonky organ fills in the manner of free jazz. The band's response was to play louder and more careeningly, raising their energy to meet and contend with his. Matthew sang with daredevil brilliance, as though shrugging off a challenge he'd never acknowledge. The song grew resolute, intractable, like some enormous watch spring that gained force the more tightly it was wound.

Now, rehearsal concluded, they drifted from the carpet toward the table. Falmouth had set out a monumental steaming bowl of bare cooked spaghetti, a quarter-stick of butter melting at its peak. The complainer hoisted bottles of wine from a rack and clapped them on the table. Matthew set to grating a brick of cheese Falmouth had thrust into his hands. Glistening blobs of tomato spattered the stove in a halo at the burner where the sauce had simmered, its savor investing through the loft. Falmouth's T-shirt was somehow spotless. Carl jerked the cork from a bottle while Falmouth elbowed past him, hands in oven mitts, to plunk the skillet between the candleholders. Matches were struck and touched to wicks, goblets splashed full, sauce ladled, Parmesan strewn to form a gooey lattice over oil-shiny plates of red-heaped noodles. Talk lulled as eating began, verbal noise replaced by a music of smacking lips, glasses clinked to teeth, the suck of spaghetti stretched by forks from pools of viscosity.

"There's both sweet and hot sausages," Falmouth lectured. "Though by now the peppered oil from the hot will have informed the entire base of the sauce. The secret ingredient is heaping spoonfuls of white sugar, more than you'd want to know about. Watch out for bay leaves, they're as sharp as shark's teeth. You've got one there, Bedwin."

"Put it here," said Denise, indicating an empty ashtray. Bedwin plucked the gleaming black leaf from the bird's nest of his pasta and held it aloft in sauce-shrouded fingers.

"All the best meals require an elephant's graveyard," said Falmouth. "Piles of shells or pits or bones. Bay leaves are like a small piece of corruption in our food, like the element of a skull in certain early Renaissance marriage paintings."

"You'd certainly never find one in a can of Chef Boyardee," said Denise.

"A bay leaf, or a skull?" said Lucinda.

"Either."

"Listen, we should have a toast," said Matthew. "It's our last rehearsal before we go on the radio. And Falmouth cooked."

"Stop eating for a minute, you greedy pigs," said Falmouth. "I propose a toast to 'Monster Eyes,' that awful song by that awful band."

"No, no," said Matthew. "To you, Falmouth. For this meal. For being our manager and spaghetti cooker."

"I've told you a hundred times, I'm not your manager. You need a proper advocate, someone who can tolerate your music."

"To Falmouth and to 'Monster Eyes' and to Bedwin, our secret genius," said Denise. "He who makes it all happen."

"Yes, to Bedwin," said Matthew. "For putting words in my mouth. May you never go solo, god help us."

"I can't sing," said Bedwin, as if he really needed to reassure them.

Lucinda, wineglass lofted, suffered a stirring of resentment. Hadn't she supplied the words to 'Monster Eyes' before their eyes? Had they suppressed all memory of the fateful rehearsal? Theirs was a band whose secret genius had a secret genius, a conspiracy huddled around a confusion. "Another toast," she blurted. "From Carl, our newest member."

The complainer was bent to his fork, connected by noodles to both teeth and plate. He ate streamingly, employing circular breathing like a horn player. Gulping, he made his eyes wide to show his willingness to speak once he'd choked down the mouthful. Matthew took up the second bottle and replenished their glasses.

"Okay, a toast," said the complainer. He stood and licked his thumb. "I like Falmouth's idea. To the stone in the cherry, the jellyfish in the lagoon, the loser among winners, the figure in the carpet, the crack in the Liberty Bell." He cleared his throat. They waited, glasses poised, uncertain he was finished. Except for Matthew, who went on eating, pointedly ignoring him. "To the tiny mouse's skull in the can of Chef Boyardee," he went on, "the one which results in a settlement of hundreds of thousands of dollars."

"Those aren't really all the same thing," said Denise.

"The jellyfish in the lagoon should be a song," said Bedwin.

"Get to work on that, you genius," muttered Matthew.

"More," said Lucinda, raptly.

"To the shark's tooth, the mouse's skull, the sour note, the sour mash, the mash note, the sour grapes, the souring of an old friendship," said the complainer. "To the resentment that hides inside love, to the loneliness that hides among companions. To bad sex."

"Watch yourself," said Falmouth. "Some of us haven't had bad sex in so long we forgot that it was bad."

"To forgetting it was bad," said the complainer, gulping back another mouthful of wine. "To telephoning an old lover and pretending to forget it was bad, to falling back into bed when you know you shouldn't, to sucking the dregs."

"You mean like a cup of coffee?"

"Exactly. The dregs of a relationship, like the dregs in a cup of coffee. To the greed of a coffee drinker for one last sip, when all that remains is a bitter sludge."

Lucinda felt gripped by an irrational jealousy. Had an old lover called him on the telephone? The instrument in question was banished to a far corner of the loft, a single ancient black enamel model with a rotary dial. It rang seldom and was answered, in Lucinda's sight, never. She'd stayed at the complainer's loft around the clock lately, up with him past dawn after rehearsals, then sleeping late into the next day, when she'd wake to find Carl preparing breakfast at two or three in the afternoon. Hardly worth returning to her apartment before the band convened again. Besides, once she'd ferried in some spare underwear and socks there was nothing to return for. After rehearsal and dinner she'd help the others pack their instruments, then escort them into the corridor and elevator. She had no wish to rub in anyone's face that she enjoyed special privileges yet no interest in hiding it, either. She felt a certain munificence in having ushered the band through so much, lyrics, gig, new member, new rehearsal space. Any trace of resentment in the others Lucinda chalked to confusion, perhaps even fear at what had overtaken them: the possibility of success. She now adopted Falmouth's attitude: most artists were their own worst enemies. As for her, she'd left hesitation behind with her apartment, her hamper full of dirty clothes, her phone blinking with who-knew-what messages. She was no longer curious what the foot sign thought. The answer to any remaining question was *yes*: yes to staying beside the complainer, yes to what she felt when she was beside him. The answer to any other question, questions to do with the band's feelings, or Matthew's, anything outside the loft and the music they made there, was: yes, quit asking. Don't imagine a broader ratification was due, from the foot sign or anywhere else. Embrace the bay leaf of the moment, which, unlike the foot sign, wasn't divided into happy and sad but was instead sweet and fearful on both of its faces.

But who called the complainer's telephone? It did ring. That he never answered it seemed to speak of the richness of his existence, and of their joint existence, now that she'd moved in with him in all but name. Other people's apartments, including her own, seemed by comparison little more than foyers for the containment of telephones, tiny shoe boxes where to ignore a call might be to lose a chance to shift oneself from the shoe box into the broader realm of human life. In the complainer's loft life was complete, so the telephone seemed negligible, a toad in a moat. Once she'd seen how he ignored it she forgave him not answering her earlier calls. Yet his phone did ring. If it had been Lucinda who was being ignored before, who was it now? Some old liaison, looking to suck dregs, or have dregs sucked?

The tall beautiful girl from the yellow chair?

The complainer was still toasting. "Just as the quality of a sporting event is determined by the level of play of the losing team, or the quality of a love affair by the way you feel when you're apart. Or of a secret, by its telling."

"I like this theory," said Falmouth. "Let me try. The quality of a restaurant meal, by the appetizers. Of a film, by its subplot."

"By the minor characters, I'd think," said Matthew.

"Bedwin went to film school," said Denise. "What is it, Bedwin, subplot or minor characters?"

He thought it over. "I had a professor who used to say that every movie had one actor you wished the whole movie was about. In a bad one you might only see them for a minute, they'd be playing a bellhop in a hotel or something. In a pretty good movie they'd have a supporting part. In a great movie you'd have the same feeling of wishing the movie was about them and they'd turn up in every scene. Right after that whoever it was would be a star in their next movie, but they'd never be as good."

"Here's another," said Falmouth. "The quality of a dinner

party is determined by the side conversations, unheard by the majority of the table."

"I don't know about that," said Matthew. "If the best talk is going on behind my back, I'm bored."

"I've got one," said Bedwin. "It's about a rock band."

No one was sure they wanted to hear the principle applied to a rock band, but it was impossible to discourage Bedwin's hard-fought attempts at conversation.

"Lay it on us," said Matthew.

"The quality of a Rolling Stones record is determined by the quality of the one song that Keith Richards sings. Like *Exile on Main Street* and "Happy" or *Some Girls* and "Before They Make Me Run.""

"Oh, no, Bedwin, that's no good at all," said Denise despairingly.

"Why not?"

"Denise thinks you're ruining the fun," said Matthew. "We were talking about universal principles and you turned it into rock trivia."

"I don't understand a word he said," said Falmouth. "Let's change the subject." He took the open bottle and topped off their glasses. Wine had no particular influence on Lucinda here, so she could drink as much as she liked. Here she was never drunk and always dreamy, as though adjusted to the intoxication of the surroundings, the roseate glow of the furniture, the imperial views of Los Angeles, so timeless and far away.

"A rock band by its worst, most incompetent member," said Carl, unexpectedly resuming, as though to salvage Bedwin's attempt. "The greatness of a song, by its worst singer."

"I'll drink to that," said Matthew distantly.

Light caught the complainer's glass as he lofted it above his ravaged spaghetti. The bell of crystal was smudged with heavy fingerprints, and bore lip-shaped gobbets of sauce around its rim. The complainer's appetite painted every clear surface it touched. I am like that glass, thought Lucinda, happily.

the cassette tape of New Zealand bands was still stuck in Matthew's player, chiming circular chords, when Lucinda opened the door of his car where he waited for her outside Carl's building, but he snapped it off defensively as she slid into her seat. The day's air was bleachy and shadowless, its temperature that of a sleeping body. Lucinda winced in the glare, bargaining with a hangover the breakfast beer she'd chugged did nothing to alleviate.

Matthew had returned Shelf the Flyer to the zoo the night before, a solo clandestine operation. His stealthiness, Lucinda supposed, formed a gesture of dignity in defeat, as well as a warning to Dr. Marian that he retained the capacity to breach her defenses. What remained today was to bring in not the animal but himself. To accept amnesty, to be allowed to resume watching over his wards and drawing a paycheck. In this perhaps more difficult hurdle he'd asked Lucinda to escort him inside, to act as witness to seal the result of her earlier negotiations. She found it impossible to say no, though as she felt the weight in the air between them she wondered, too late, if the request had as much to do with a wish to bear her away from Carl's loft. It was Lucinda's first time outside the loft in most of a week. As they drove to the zoo in perfect silence she felt the whining surface of the highway through the Mazda's flimsy chassis. Restored to ground level, she felt antlike, exposed, alarmed.

Arrived, they strolled among the exhibits, browsing incognito on the eucalyptus-littered paths. In the noon sun the zoo resembled a tray of compartments that had been shaken and plunked back to earth by some careless child, the inhabitants of each exhibit dizzy, pressing themselves to the walls or bars of their enclosures as if expecting to be lifted and shaken again. A hyena rolled its eyes at them, begging with a sideways tongue. Three giraffes bunched as if tethered at the ankles. Woolly goats teetered in gutters.

They found the false outback full of kangaroos, sprawled in textbook melancholia. Lucinda couldn't tell at a glance whether Shelf was among them, or instead segregated in some kind of debriefing room elsewhere.

"Is she there?" Lucinda asked.

"Don't you recognize her?"

"No," she admitted.

So the episode ended, Shelf blending into the population at last. Matthew gazed stoically. No kangaroo returned his gaze. Perhaps Shelf had been cured of expectations after all.

The zoo offices, warned by Shelf's reappearance, had seemingly been made ready for Matthew's return. Though he crept in braced for ambush, the girl at the desk greeted him blithely. Lucinda waved and smiled, compensating for Matthew's glum demeanor. Other vets or orderlies in white coats passed through, hailing him in friendly tones. He only grunted, clearing out his mailbox, sifting the recyclable memos into a bin, pocketing sealed envelopes. Then they turned to Dr. Marian's office. There lay the one severe test.

"Mr. Plangent." The zoo director turned her barrel-chested authority from her paperwork and scrutinized the two of them, her deep-pocketed eyes glistening.

"Dr. Marian. You're looking well."

"And yourself. But enough pleasantries. We've got creatures that require your attention." Dr. Marian slapped a pile of folders that might have been prepared for this moment. "Duncan needs his claws recauterized, first thing."

"Duncan?"

"The Taiwanese lynx. You remember."

"Sure, sure."

"And there's a tenacious rhinovirus among the tufted capuchins. Just the two-year-olds."

"We've seen that before."

"Indeed we have."

"I'll schedule in some dropper work on their sinuses."

"I never doubted you would."

"I'll just have to drive my friend home first, and get my locker key."

"That's fine."

"Thank you."

Lucinda felt invisible, a bystander to codes that had no need of her presence. She turned to leave, still unacknowledged, but Dr. Marian said, "Ms. Hoekke?"

"Yes?"

"I listened to the tape you sent me."

Lucinda had almost forgotten. She waited, not wishing to presume.

"Some of it was very interesting."

"It's just a rehearsal tape. If we recorded in a studio the results would be much better."

"Nonetheless, I found much to like. I'm still not clear on how you envision my role, however."

Matthew busied himself examining the stack of files, displaying absolute neutrality, an unwillingness even to show surprise in this instance.

"There are, uh, elements which have shown an interest in the band," said Lucinda. "Not exactly preying, but putting themselves forward obtrusively. Middle-aged men of a certain stripe. I somehow pictured that you might—keep them in line. Give us some breathing room."

"Yes, I see." Dr. Marian left no uncertainty that she was aware of the power deriving from her inverted pyramidal form and ramrod posture, from the white stripe in her raven hair. Male guilt crackled around her like Frankensteinian electricity.

"We're playing live on the radio on Friday," said Lucinda. "Four in the afternoon, on KPKD, a show called *The Dreaming Jaw*. You could come and observe."

"I'll have to clear some things on my schedule."

"We'd be grateful."

Lucinda and Matthew continued unspeaking back through the maze of the zoo, pausing over no animals, stalking their way to the parking lot. Matthew walked slightly ahead, perhaps managing embarrassment. No words passed between them until he tucked his Mazda under the curbside shadow of the Olive Street tower.

"You seem ticked at me," said Lucinda.

"This whole thing's just a little strange, that's all."

"What whole thing?"

Matthew glanced at the building, perhaps about to name the complainer, then thought better of it. "Just the way everything is totally rearranged and exactly the same. It's depressing to see Shelf back inside. You know that feeling of wondering if something ever really happened? Of wondering if something was ever real in the first place?"

"It's all real, Matthew."

"I know."

"You don't like my new friend, that's what you mean."

"I like your new friend a lot, actually. I do think he looks a little fat onstage with the rest of us. I guess I'm not supposed to say that."

"He's not fat, he's just a grown-up. We're the ones who look strange. We're anorexic, we're ghosts, we're tinder."

"I thought we looked pretty good."

"You don't like him."

"If there's anything I don't like it's his effect on you. The way you act. I probably wasn't supposed to say that, either."

"You can say whatever you want."

"Well, here's one thing. I hope you never felt I was trying to suck dregs, or that there was any aspect of dreg-sucking going on between you and me, because I never did, not once."

"I never felt that at all."

"No matter how many times we broke up and then called each other late at night and then ended up in bed together again, I would never have described anything between us as a dreg suck."

"I promise you, neither would I."

"I don't want to screw up anything with the band. I'm very excited about Friday."

"So am I. You're not screwing anything up, Matthew. Nothing could be screwed up."

"Thanks for helping me today, Lucinda, I really appreciate it, and Shelf does too. I think I'm going to drive away now, if you want to get out of the car."

t he radio station's unglamour was sobering. No one would have pictured Fancher Autumnbreast, paragon of bohemian taste, amid the bland commercial edifices and slickly nostalgic boutiques and dozy, off-brand policemen of Culver City. The band converged on Duquesne Avenue in three cars: Bedwin with Denise, Carl driving Lucinda's Datsun, Matthew alone. Now they stood assembled in the vanilla-carpeted lobby of the station's studio as if dragged into the day's light for a medical procedure. Their misspelled names checked off in an appointment book by an unimpressed receptionist, they were led upstairs and abandoned to a greenroom full of surfing and cigar magazines, bottled water, and wicker cornucopia full of bruised grapes, coagulated brie, and sesame crackers.

"I'd like to explode a place like this with a bomb, if it could be okay to say that."

"You need to build up your immunity. If we rocket to the top it'll require a series of compromises with antiseptic environments."

"Shouldn't we have brought spray paint or a television set to push out a window?"

"I don't think you're supposed to destroy a television set at a radio station."

They glimpsed Autumnbreast only momentarily, a figure in a gray sweat suit with orange piping. He hailed them with a vigorous bout of silent winking and finger-snapping through a large window as they set up their instruments in a crowded booth. Only the complainer seemed free of the pall that eclipsed the group, the apprehension that they were the wrong band with the wrong song. They feared that they might be unready, or the opposite: they might be over-practiced, fallen out of synch, and had ruined the song. Maybe they'd gotten out of the wrong sides of their beds. Wasn't four in the afternoon, anyway, a famous energy sink, a vortex of enervated human attention? Who would listen to the song, who would care? Or perhaps they'd arrived at the wrong time in the history of *The Dreaming Jaw* to make clear use of its indisputable influence on musical fashion. Maybe they'd even been tricked. This wasn't the real KPKD, or the real Autumnbreast, but some obscure counterfeit. While they blunderingly tuned instruments in a glass-and-foam booth in Culver City some other band enjoyed glory that belonged rightly to them, in some other place that felt more encouragingly real.

The complainer, exempt, jabbered. "Do you know why people fall out of love in small apartments?" he said, apropos of nothing. "Because they can't gaze at each other over a large enough distance. You need to be able to watch the other person as if you weren't there to be seen yourself, like sighting a creature in the forest."

"Who did you fall out of love with in a small apartment?" Lucinda asked. She felt as though Carl spooled from her, an astronaut outside the space station, drifting on his tether.

"Nobody. I mean, lots of people. When I was married I lived in a basement apartment in San Francisco."

"You were married?" said Denise.

"About a million years ago. Another era, like prehistory. The Susan Ming Dynasty."

Matthew and Bedwin went on plinking at their instruments, testing microphone levels for the engineer on the far side of the glass, a blasé goth girl with lank black hair and a nocturnally pale complexion, a silver ring piercing one eyebrow. Her own mike channel bled into their booth, ceaseless incomprehensible staticky asides directed to unseen others.

"Was your wife's name Susan Ming?" Lucinda whispered to the complainer. Before he could answer they were overwhelmed by Fancher Autumnbreast's looming passage into the booth. Autumnbreast squinted his mournful brow as if across some great distance, though the tiny booth barely contained him and the band. Despite the tracksuit he gave off traces of patchouli and clove, redolent smoke. Shaking his leonine head and showing the slightest of smiles he embraced Matthew. Then he reached for Lucinda, kissing each cheek and tipping her elegantly, fingertips at the small of her back, like a Flamenco dancer. Bedwin he chucked under the chin. Bedwin blushed. Autumnbreast then blew a kiss to Denise, his gesture fulsome. The four quivered slightly, puppyish under his hand.

"Oh, you dizzy kids." He squinted one eye, a wink stilled to a sardonic frieze. The band waited, enspelled. Finally Autumnbreast lifted his chin at the complainer, who stood grinning at his keyboard. "Who he?" he asked Matthew.

"New band member," said the complainer, sticking out his hand. "Carl's the name."

Autumnbreast squinted more deeply, suggesting the complainer was difficult to make out, a form vanishing in wavering heat lines on far asphalt. "Hmmm," he said.

"Yes?" said the complainer.

"Fifth Beatle," said Autumnbreast.

"Ten minutes," warned the buzzing voice of the engineer. Lucinda looked up to discover Jules Harvey standing at the glass, slightly behind the goth girl at her board, peering in at them pleasantly from beneath his baseball cap. Who'd notified him of their appointment here? Not Denise, surely. Perhaps Matthew or Bedwin had fallen under his bland spell. Or Fancher Autumnbreast might have been plugging their appearance in advance, so Harvey might have heard it on the radio.

Autumnbreast widened his hands. "Everybody beautiful?"

They gawped, perplexed.

"You're miked?"

"They're miked," the engineer cut in.

"Then you're beautiful," said Autumnbreast, as though knighting them with the scepter of his esteem. "Except you, Beatle. What do you do?"

"Play this keyboard, sir."

"Sing?"

"I do, sir."

Autumnbreast shook his head, sighed, furrowed, pursed. "Goof."

"Sorry?"

"You heard me, Beatle." Autumnbreast repeated the word silently, as in a game of charades, pointing from himself to the complainer.

"I think I understand," said Carl.

"Doctor, heal thyself," said Autumnbreast.

"Seven minutes," said the engineer.

"Are we being interviewed?" interrupted Denise, speaking in her confusion for the whole band. "Or just playing the song?"

"Yes."

"Uh, yes what?"

"This gig's easy, pumpkin. I tickle you, and you laugh."

"Excuse me?"

"Be organic," said Autumnbreast, pained to explain.

"Just speak into your mikes," explained the engineer. "Try not to pop your plosives or say fuck or shit. I probably ought to get a quick sound check to balance the instruments, Mr. Autumnbreast." Other figures now joined the engineer behind the glass, fitting themselves along the wall on either side of Jules Harvey: Rhodes Bramlett of Considerable Records, and Mick Felsh in his cowboy shirt. Bramlett and Felsh offered small gesticulations and nods of encouragement to the band once they were spotted, as if to say, *Don't mind us.*

The complainer raised his hand. "Sir?"

"Yes, Beatle?"

"Our guitarist needs a chair."

"Chair."

Bedwin nodded shamefully.

"And," the complainer went on, "I think I'd prefer to lie on the floor."

"Are you sick?" asked Denise.

"No, it's for the song. Can we put the microphone on the floor?"

"You want to sing on the floor?" said Matthew.

"I need to sing on the floor, yes."

"You won't be able to play the keyboard," said Denise.

"You don't need me on keyboard."

No one could argue that point.

"I need to be on the floor to get the right emotion. I've just had a realization, that I wasn't giving the band my all. Art requires sacrifice, even of one's dignity."

Lucinda loved most of all his careening integrity to his impulses, even if he might seem to be careening away from her. She would have played her bass on the floor if only to be beside him. But even if it was possible, there wasn't room.

"Six minutes," said the engineer. "I better get a sound check."

Everyone waited for Autumnbreast, who said at last, "Mike Beatle on the floor, Morsel."

"Thank you," said Carl. "And a chair for Bedwin."

"And a chair."

The engineer Autumnbreast had called Morsel tramped from behind her instrument panel, through the rubber-sealed doors, which opened with a sound like a sneeze, and into the sound booth. She rearranged the complainer's mike stand, loosening the hinge and capsizing the microphone so it hovered a few inches from the carpet. She was pure efficiency, a human clock ticking toward their on-air deadline. The band could only watch, reduced to an autistic helplessness. Fancher Autumnbreast sat cross-legged against the lip of the booth's window, his back to Harvey, Bramlett, and Felsh, bridging his forehead with his fingers, radiating philosophical detachment from all present events.

"Try this," said Morsel.

The complainer threaded his sneakered feet through Denise's

kit, laid his right arm under Lucinda's mike stand, and settled his bulk across the cables that ribboned the carpet. Jules Harvey tapped on the window of the glass booth and mouthed inaudible suggestions. Rhodes Bramlett came through the door with a folding chair, which Matthew passed to Bedwin, who settled on it like a dog for a nap, tucking one foot under his thigh, curling the other into the chair's struts and himself around his guitar. Bramlett didn't depart, but instead squatted low against the wall, hiding behind Matthew. He raised a finger to his lips, pleading with the band not to finger him to Autumnbreast, who hadn't seemed to register the A&R man's intrusion. Mick Felsh, on the other side, looked perturbed that Bramlett had achieved this coup. He leaned in to whisper to Harvey, who remained serene.

Morsel scurried past Autumnbreast, through the sound-sealed door, and reseated at her control panel. Autumnbreast, like a human buttress, revealed no trace of urgency. His wide hand now fully masked his face, thumb and fingertips over his eyes, Hamlet with a headache.

"Three minutes," said Morsel on the PA. "Everybody want to give me a little something? First, uh, the person on the floor."

"I'm the man who wrote 'Monster Eyes,' " began the complainer from the floor, in falsetto, as if improvising a new song, about himself.

"Okay, that's fine," interrupted Morsel. "Lead vocal, I grabbed your levels already. Chair guy, play a chord or two." The engineer circumnavigated the room, eliciting twangs and mumbles. "Fair enough, sounds good, sounds good . . . Mr. Autumnbreast, we should probably get you into the booth."

Autumnbreast turned and looked at her as if startled.

"One minute, sir," said Morsel apologetically.

"Sure," said Autumnbreast, coming out of his trance. "Okee-doke, kittens. This is radio."

The band waited to understand.

"You won't see me," said Autumnbreast, "but I'm with you, all over and through you."

"Give them the pep talk," said Morsel on the PA.

"Pep talk."

"They're nervous, I believe."

"Okeedoke. Listen. Million bands have done the *Jaw*. Here's what I say. Secret to radio is, think of your favorite person. Got a favorite person?"

"Alex Chilton," said Bedwin.

Autumnbreast winced. "Only think, not say."

"Sorry."

"Chilton set fire to my wallet," mused Autumnbreast. "Paris, 1974. Marianne was there. Trying to impress her."

"Thirty seconds, sir."

"You were saying think of our favorite person," nudged Matthew.

"Sure, dandelion. Favorite person. When you talk, pretend you're them. Only it can't be me. Because that's who I'm pre-tending to be."

"The booth, sir."

Autumnbreast offered them one last expansive gaze, then swept out. Rhodes Bramlett remained wedged to one side of the window. Perhaps Bramlett was beneath consideration, a rat free to scurry where he liked. Silence enveloped the room. Even Morsel's buzzing dimmed as she bore down on her instrument panel. Jules Harvey stood behind her, head cocked like a terrier.

Denise tightened the wing nut on her lone cymbal, her brow furrowed, presenting musicianly integrity in the face of any circum-
stance. Bedwin appeared to be licking or gnawing his frets.
Matthew postured at his mike stand, perhaps attempting to re-
capture an attitude essential to putting the song across, perhaps
even trying out Autumnbreast's advice. Who was Matthew's favorite person? Lucinda had never known, a sad thought. The
complainer lay with his eyes closed, possibly asleep. His shirt
gaped at the buttons, permitting sproutage of unruly hairs. He
looked essential, sexual, a fistlike ruddy bulb planted in the gar-
den of the band.

"Three, two, one," counted Morsel softly.

"Welcome," came Fancher Autumnbreast's voice. As he'd
promised them, he was invisible, yet everywhere at once. He
purred through the room, intoned in their bodies like a bass line.
"Back. Me Jaw, You Dreaming. Wide-awake Dreaming. So. Here.
Guests. Rare. Debut. Silver Lake. Echo Park. Friends. We've
Heard. You've Heard. You'll Hear. They're Playing. For You, Live.
They Were Four, Now They're Five. Changes Already."

Into the silence that followed came the profound, ear-
ringing emptiness of outer space.

"MONSTER EYES," said Fancher Autumnbreast. "Real
Sweetheart People."

At that moment it was unmistakable. Something had re-
solved from their miasmic hesitation, the band had been named.
Fancher Autumnbreast had only to pronounce the syllables,
publish them into the ether. Monster Eyes was the banner under which they flew, had perhaps always been so, without them
knowing.

"Talk to Los Angeles, Monster Eyes."

Nobody spoke.

"When, Bunnyrabbits. Where. Names. Influences. Are You Recording or Touring."

Starting with Matthew and ending with Carl they each spoke their names, gave faltering hellos and thank yous.

"Met. How."

"Matthew and I were working at a copy shop together."

"She and Denise played in a band in school."

"We always thought Bedwin was so talented."

"I dialed a number I found stickered on a pay phone—"

"The Song," interrupted Autumnbreast.

They were stopped again.

"Big Party, Major Scene. Everybody Knows Harvey. Jules Harvey. Slayed the Crowd. People Talking."

"It's ironic, actually, because we were originally meant to play silently—"

"Played It Twice. First Time, Ecstasy. Second Time, Fear."

"Sorry?"

"I Fear You, Monster Eyes."

"Uh, thanks a lot, that really means a lot to us, coming from you."

"Who."

"What?"

"Wrote It. The Anthem. The Howl."

Simultaneously Bedwin said "Lucinda," Lucinda said "Carl," and Denise said "Bedwin." The complainer, from the floor, said nothing.

"Group Mind. That's Who."

Through the glass, Lucinda saw Jules Harvey leaning nearer to Morsel, as though to guide the movements of her hands on the control panel with his eyes. He was in the grip of his fetish, sniffing the engineer's armpit. Lucinda wanted to shout out a warning, but stifled it helplessly. Mick Felsh, staring avidly through the glass at the band, paid no attention.

Inside the booth, Rhodes Bramlett, still in his feral huddle, produced a pocket tape recorder. He held it half concealed in his cupped hands, tiny red indicator blinking under his chin. He was ready to stealthily record the song, perhaps for a bootleg release, or else to copyright the lyrics and chord changes, a legal obligation he'd brandish over the band until it ended in court. Again Lucinda throttled a cry.

"Unfetter Your Charisma," said Autumnbreast. "Los Angeles Is Suffering to Hear You, Monster Eyes."

"Sorry?" said Matthew.

"Sing Your Song."

"First I want to explain something," said the complainer. "Before we sing. If that's okay."

"Newest Member," said Autumnbreast. "Lucky Man."

"I do feel lucky, yes, thank you," said the complainer.

"On the Studio Floor. Like a Drowned Eagle."

"That's what I wanted to explain. It came to me today that 'Monster Eyes' is really a song about death. The singer of the song is sort of a zombie, issuing a warning to the living."

"Zombie."

"Monster Eyes is really the force that degrades every living thing," said the complainer. "When you look at the world or another person through monster eyes you're sensing the putrefaction in beautiful things, the spoiled vegetables and tumors and decaying teeth, the funky odors that cling even to babies and beautiful women—"

The band was frozen. Lucinda spoke as if in a nightmare, to intervene. "I think what Carl means is that when you don't love someone . . . you're prone to . . . there's a certain kind . . ."

"Some Things Don't."

"Sorry?" said Lucinda, into the aching loud silence.

Autumnbreast hadn't finished his thought. He continued: "Need. Saying."

"I'm not entirely sure we ought to play this song anymore," said the complainer. "Maybe since we've come all this way, just one last time. But we should sing it honestly, like zombies, since it's a zombie song."

Autumnbreast's Oz-like voice emitted the sole syllable with which he'd earlier indicted the complainer in person: "Goof."

"That's why I'm lying on the floor, so I can give it a more sepulchral voice-from-the-grave kind of sound."

Denise had been silent since speaking her name. Now she raised her sticks and ticked off the song's beat, voting for a musical escape from their interview. It was what Autumnbreast had requested, after all: their song. Bedwin fell in, lightly riffing the chord. It wasn't the intro they'd rehearsed, but the song's form was recognizable, though threadbare. Rhodes Bramlett grinned and aimed his tiny recorder. On the other side of the glass, Morsel stretched her open palms toward the ceiling in sinuous alternation, opening her armpits for Jules Harvey's nosing study, her eyelids shut and lips pouted as she basked in the attention. Farther back, Mick Felsh had retreated into the shadows, where he consulted with another figure. Was it Autumnbreast, returned to admire their song? Felsh's hands were clasped at his chest. He appeared to be apologizing to or pleading with this new form in the darkness.

Lucinda curled two fingers down to flesh the ghostlike song with her bass line. The complainer began to bark out the song's first lyrics, Matthew's opening lines, only in a garbled and deranged form. "Better conceal yourself from the light, oooh, my little pumpkin . . . there are things that come out at night, and they come out galumphing . . . um, I'm the one who'll always cut you down to size . . . ah, excavating your flaws with my monstrous eyes, wow . . ." The microphone Morsel had set on the floor was well placed, capturing the complainer's every hissed sibilant.

"Wait, wait—" Denise quit the beat, so the music unspooled, Bedwin's chords reduced to choppy nonsense. "Carl, what are you doing?"

"Well—"

"That's Matthew's part. And you're singing it wrong."

"I'm improvising." Flat on the floor as if gazing at clouds, the complainer remained blithe. It was as though they were trying to wake a dreamer, demanding he rise and walk. Or maybe the rest of them, destroying their chances on live radio, late for the party that was meant to be their lives, gone to school without pants, were the dreamers.

"You can't do that now," said Denise.

"It's my song," he said. "Matthew can sing it with me."

"It's not your song. You didn't even write those lyrics, Lucinda did."

The shadowy form on the far side of the glass made itself apparent. Dr. Marian. All in black up to her turtleneck collar, she seemed a floating array of white hands and face and skunk's hairstreak, a dervish of authority. Mick Felsh had been banished from the control room. Now she confronted Jules Harvey. Startled from his pheremonal intoxication, he didn't stand a chance. The bright disks of his glasses lenses bobbed as he nodded in reply to Dr. Marian's rebuke. Dr. Marian pointed to the door, making his sole option apparent. Morsel returned to fiddling dials, looking somewhat chagrined, her paleness flawed with color high in her cheeks and at her throat.

"Let's try again," said Lucinda hopelessly. "Matthew, maybe if you just sing—"

Denise ticked at her drum again, daring them to follow. Lucinda thrummed the bass figure. Rhodes Bramlett nodded approval. He, at least, was undiscouraged. Bedwin, though, had cinched both feet on the lip of his chair, knees twinned as though to protect his guitar from attack. Autumnbreast's voice was conspicuous in its absence now, and no sign, encouraging or otherwise, came from Morsel.

"Carl, will you promise not to come in before Matthew?" said Denise.

"I promise to embrace the song and everything I feel, and everything you feel, too." He lay immobile, his belly rising and falling with his breath. His voice filled the room, seeming endless, self-sustaining, horrible, the same voice that had once blazed its trail inside Lucinda, across Falmouth's complaint line. Now she seemed to behold it from a million miles away, as if a comet in her sky, tail shedding interstellar slush and gravel in the guise of heat and light, now passed through to some other, colder night. "Maybe we should sing it a cappella," he continued. "Or recite it like a one-act play, which might help bring out the drama in the words—"

Dr. Marian came through the door and stood spotlit in the band's midst. Her prowlike chest and chin, her front-heavy bun of hair, nearly a pompadour, her flashing, careworn eyes, all demanded their absolute attention. Even Rhodes Bramlett scrambled to his feet, as though already under indictment. Dr. Marian only scowled at Bramlett once, and waved him to the exit. He slinked off.

"Mr. Plangent," Dr. Marian said. "Ms. Hoekke."

No one spoke.

"I begin to see the problem."

"You do?" said Lucinda.

"It's unmistakable. Mr. Vogelsong—am I saying that right?"

"That's my name. Who are you?"

"That's not important right now. May I see you outside, Mr. Vogelsong?"

The complainer was silent. No one rescued him from the cooling clarity of Dr. Marian's request. He flounced on the tiles, his white hair sloppy, his posture poor even lying on his back, taking up uncommon amounts of space and air. Dr. Marian stood, bulletlike, arms crossed under her breasts, *Monitor* challenging *Merrimac*.

"Do I have to?" he said at last.

"Yes. You've come to an end here, Mr. Vogelsong."

"If you say so."

"I do."

"You're a hard woman to refuse." A certain lascivious quality flickered in his tone, pointlessly. He batted his lids at her, upside down.

"Don't flatter yourself. You don't know me that well."

"I'm sorry."

"Apology accepted." She pointed at the door.

He giggled, feebly.

Dr. Marian was less the band's new manager than a figure of death, it seemed to Lucinda. The complainer had invoked the word and she'd come in black to collect him. Now he squirmed onto his stomach and crawled from amid the band's equipment, making a path around Matthew's mike stand. Dr. Marian held open the rubber-sealed door. The complainer remained on all fours, his expression that of a supplicant. She offered a curt nod as he passed over the threshold and continued down the corridor, padding along the carpet beneath rows of framed photographs of local luminaries. Dr. Marian went after him with a crisp air of unfinished business. The door sealed behind her.

The room was restored to silence, underlined by the ambient hum of their amplified unplayed guitars. Morsel sat silent, framed at her console in the control room. She met them with a level, not-unfriendly gaze. Matthew coughed resoundingly, his back to the others. The coils of Denise's snare rattled in sympathy with the cough. Lucinda swayed hips and instrument rightward, filling some of the space the complainer had vacated. She imagined she could sense the warmth of the complainer's absented weight through the soles of her sneakers, but it was surely only foolish imagination. Even if so, it was felt only by her. It was otherwise as if they'd come to this room without him. They made a foursome again, a band utterly changed by having accommodated the complainer, having binged on his lyrics and his apartment, yet, embarrassingly, still themselves: Denise, fixed at her set, emanating resolve; Bedwin, clinging to his instrument's neck for solace; Matthew, infinitely damaged and proud, without even a guitar to disguise his singer's fear of irrelevance; Lucinda, negotiating between, medium for the band's yearning and confusion, their betrayer and fool, their bass player.

Denise now stirred them with a beat, metronomically clean. Lucinda fitted her bass notes around the drum's tick. Bedwin joined too, his chords a perfect emanation from his hiding place, his nerd's gauze of self. There was only a held breath at the point when Matthew ought to have come in and didn't. The singer stood making himself ready, seeming to weigh the band and the song with his shoulders. They bypassed him to play an instrumental verse, an overture. He met the song at the second pass. Lucinda had never heard him sing this way. She thought she heard a measure of the complainer's tormented yawp in his approach, as though he'd subsumed Carl's voice in his own. It didn't matter. It was the best they ever played.

Morsel tiptoed out when no one was looking, so when they finished they were entirely alone. Autumnbreast didn't speak if he was listening. It was hard to believe he'd heard. No one congratulated them, no one was on the line, no one had broadcast or bootlegged their small, enraptured song. They waited in the booth in dumb embarrassment until Morsel reappeared. She offered them release forms, which they signed without reading.

"We weren't on the radio, were we?"

"Just the first part of the interview," said Morsel. "After that the station went to a cart, a prerecorded feature on Mr. Autumnbreast's charitable work with rescued greyhounds who worked at racetracks, including his own companion animal, Verve."

"Not the song."

"Not the song."

"Thank you."

"Good luck."

Matthew walked Lucinda out. Denise and Bedwin were

already gone. Lucinda's car was where she'd left it, but Carl had her key. They abandoned it, rode in an elevator to the top of a parking garage to Matthew's Mazda and loaded Lucinda's bass into the backseat. He turned the key in the ignition, then stopped, staring across the roof at a tall figure folding his legs into a small sports car.

They walked over. Fancher Autumnbreast seemed to wait for them. There was no companion animal in the car, a canvas-topped convertible Porsche with a leather brassiere cupping its headlamps.

"Pretty," said Autumnbreast, once Lucinda and Matthew stood at his driver's window. His expression was fond and wounded, resigned as if to inevitable historical forces, famine, genocide, tyranny.

"Sorry?"

"You're pretty."

"We wanted to apologize."

Autumnbreast lifted his hands from the wheel, shut his eyes.

"Will you have us back on the show?"

Autumnbreast blinked, tried to find words. "Who?"

"Us. Monster Eyes."

Autumnbreast smiled forgivingly.

"What you saw in us before, it can't be completely gone," said Matthew.

Autumnbreast raised a fist as though in solidarity, curled it to his own lips, and kissed each of his four knuckles, his eyes again gently lidded.

"Are you saying it's gone?" demanded Lucinda.

Autumnbreast sighed, seeming to wish they could interpret

his gnomic gesture and spare themselves the squalor of mere language. Seeing their wide waiting eyes, he spoke.

"It's so gone, buttermilk, it's like it was never there."

She only understood that she'd fallen asleep and where when his telephone rang, a whirr or chortle you'd produce by great effort with a hand-cranked eggbeater. She opened her eyes. Orange zones of lamplight glowed throughout the loft, the kitchen counters lit like a derrick at sea. The bed too glowed within its green curtain, another outpost she must have lit during her initial circuit, an attempt to lure him back by bringing his apartment to life. The turntable's needle crackled, endlessly reinscribing the loose spiral between an LP's final song and its label, a subliminal noise mimicking a cricket's call. Matthew had dropped Lucinda here hours ago. Her car was still in Culver City unless the complainer had returned there with her key to drive it.

In an ALL THINKING IS WISHFUL T-shirt and holey underwear she sprawled in a large paisley chair, her bare knees cradling a two-thirds empty bottle of scotch. Her mouth tasted of drink. She scratched her calf where it had wrinkled hotly against the chair's arm. Two of her fingers were stuck together.

She'd meant to masturbate, was pretty certain she'd failed.

The black laminate telephone gargled a second time, reposing its problem.

Lucinda gaped at it stupidly. Really, the holes were so small she doubted the complainer's clubby fingers could fit in them. But she was being confused: you could answer a telephone you never dialed. Not that she'd ever seen him do either. But it might be him calling. He might know she'd come here and be cuddling this bottle with her thighs in a chair, curled beside the telephone as if she was seeking its warmth.

The phone seemed to take months between rings, allowing agonies of indecision, and now she was sure it had stopped. But no, it rang again. She worked to remoisten a snoring tongue dried to clay against back molars.

"Hello?" The receiver was a carpenter's C-clamp she pressed to one side of her face. She gripped her right wrist with her left hand for support.

"Uh, hello," said a young woman's voice. "Is Carl there?"

"No."

"Oh, okay."

"He'll be right back. I can take a message."

"Oh, thanks, I'll call another time."

"Do you have a yellow chair?"

"Excuse me?"

"Is your name Susan Ming?"

The caller hung up.


She woke desperate to pee at six when the uncovered window flooded the complainer's loft with sky, the lamps still lit, Lucinda still in her chair, the bottle drained. She showered and left her damp towels where they fell, dressed in the previous day's clothes, then burned herself trying to operate his espresso machine, her sole former art now eluding her. She settled instead for a remedial beer, the chill bottle relief for her scorched thumb. In shame she called no one for a lift, paid a cab instead to take her to Culver City to rendezvous with a locksmith at her parked car. It was barely eight in the morning, the streets brightly vacant.

"What happened to your car?" asked the locksmith, nodding at the crinkled bumper, still fresh enough to raise notice, the metal raw where the paint had crackled.

"It bumped into something," said Lucinda.

Her Datsun recaptured, she piloted home. The car limped, as though it had accommodated to the complainer's mass, his breakneck lefts full of body English and swearing. She parked and slugged to the door of her scorned apartment, exhausted in nine a.m. sunlight. Unlike the car, Lucinda's rooms weren't marked by the complainer's use, his cavalier hands, but instead by her own neglect, a habitat she'd molted like a shell. She crept in, averting her gaze from the slaw of mail beneath the door slot and the answering machine's blinking message counter. She avoided any glimpse of the foot sign, too, uninterested in its smug fateful knowledge. What she wanted was to hear the complainer coming again, overspilling himself against her breasts, mumbling his gratitude, moving southward to finish her. She slid between her old bed's stale crumby layers and dozed in melancholy.

She kept herself from returning to Olive Street until after dark, just, though she dialed his number a half-dozen times waiting. The foot sign, when she at last glanced, was out of order, its fuse blown or gears jammed. Her view was of its stilled edge bisecting the pale wash of dusk above Sunset, no foot to be seen, sick or healthy. She called the clinic to complain, but the foot doctors weren't picking up the phone either. Los Angeles was the largest inhabited abandoned city on earth.

She drove back under a spell of apprehension. It was as if she and the band had fallen into a void, dead air, somewhere between the last digits of Morsel's countdown and the zero of their own thwarted possibilities. As for Carl, Lucinda only wanted him back, wanted once more to be tickled and fooled and swallowed, be made undisappointed and whole. Nothing more. She examined the bumpers of neighboring cars for his slogans, the words he'd moaned in her ear and hidden in plain view throughout the world, but couldn't find any.

She discovered him there behind the green curtain, packing a black leather case that sat open on his bed. Toothbrush and underwear, nothing else, gear for an astronaut's departure, or a child's sleepover. He rolled his shaggy head at the sound of her entrance. The lamps she'd lit still blazed. Her damp towels still lay crumpled like tribute at his feet. Yet nothing in the loft belonged to her, unless it was the pile of Falmouth's drawings of the band, drooping ignored over the hood of the pinball machine in the distant corner. The drawings spoke of her life before this disaster, far from this place.

"Where are you going?"

"I'd like to avoid feeling guilty if that's at all possible."

"You don't need to feel guilty, just explain."

"There's someone else."

"I saw." The truth fell on her like injurious rain: she already knew.

"Yes," he agreed. "You were there when it happened."

"Did you and Dr. Marian know each other from before?"

"No. I've never met anyone like her."

"That's beautiful," said Lucinda, trying to keep the bitterness from her voice.

"You can stay here if you want," he said. He struggled to zipper the tiny case with his mittenlike hands. "I don't know when I'll be back, but in the meantime I'd be thrilled if you and the band made use of the place."

"You don't want to be in the band anymore?"

"Marian thinks I should simplify. Anyway, I really wasn't helping things, was I?"

"I thought you were proud of the songs." Lucinda knew she'd begun sulking.

"The songs are great. But it's just not really my kind of thing, trying to be liked. For instance, I really screwed up the radio show."

Lucinda astonished herself by saying, "I thought it went okay."

"You're being kind."

"I was here before," she said. "I answered the telephone, I hope that's okay. I have a message for you."

"Yes?"

"Susan Ming called."

"Who's Susan Ming?"

Lucinda felt in a panic that she'd had nothing to drink, was hopelessly sober. The world, unenlivened by alcohol or music or sex, was tinny, pallid, unwound. She felt starved for the complainer's talk, his language that once seemed capable of saying anything and now appeared capable of saying nothing. No language could tell what she knew at this moment: that she'd loved the complainer more than she'd ever managed to say.

"I must have gotten the name wrong," she said at last.

"Or it was a wrong number," he said helpfully.

"There's something you said before," she began, wanting to break through to him, to remind him of their language. "That a genius of sex was a terrible thing to be—"

"To *only* be," he corrected. "Anyway, I think I called it sad, not terrible, although that would probably make a better lyric in a song."

"Please be serious with me," she cried.

He opened his palms. "This part of my life isn't serious."

"Which part is?"

"There is no other part."

She fled.


Matthew wasn't home. It was too late for the zoo, but without the kangaroo pinning him to his apartment he was freed to his nightclub crawling, his life full of bands he was shocked Lucinda had never heard of. She drove to Denise's apartment, knocked. Nothing. The windows were dark. She tried No Shame, feeling sordid and guilty among the evening clientele, the couples browsing videos. Denise wasn't at the counter. Lucinda asked the clerk, who said Denise wasn't on again until tomorrow. Then mentioned he'd seen the show at Jules Harvey's loft. How he'd loved it, especially that one song.

Were Matthew and Denise together? Possibly the whole band was together, apart from her. She'd let the universe slide into ruin while she frolicked with the complainer, and now anything was possible, even likely. She drove to Falmouth's gallery, but the doors were locked, the window dark. Cars whistled past on Sunset, Saturday night under way.

Lucinda hadn't visited Falmouth at home for years. She barely recalled where he lived. She couldn't ambush him there now in desperation. He might mock her distress. Or worse, be sincere, and sketch her. It was the band she needed. Monster Eyes, the dreamers, the fools, her only friends.

She appeared at Bedwin's cottage door without offering this time, no pizza, no yellow pages of cribbed lyrics, only a bottle of scotch as good as that she'd drained at the complainer's, acquired at the Pink Elephant in defiant nostalgia. She cracked the seal on the bottle at the curb in front of Bedwin's steps and slugged a shot straight from its lip. Bedwin was home, of course. He opened the door to his converted garage, his secret grotto, in a T-shirt, blue-piped at neck and biceps, with the words BIG STAR emblazoned on his sweet puny chest.

"What are you doing?" Lucinda demanded, before he could ask it of her.

"Just watching a movie," Bedwin said helplessly, as though he knew it was an indefensible reply.

"That's funny because it's the same thing you were doing the last time I visited you, remember? When I came with the lyrics?"

"Sure, Lucinda, I remember."

"You're not watching the same movie, are you?" She peered past Bedwin's shoulder at the screen, winking like an electric eye from his cavern of stuff. On it, a jocular engineer beckoned from the narrow window of a massive locomotive. "Something about choo-choos?"

"*Human Desire*, by Fritz Lang."

"The one you've watched, like, a hundred times."

"Not a hundred, but yes, that's right."

"Can I come in?"

"Do you have more lyrics?" His tone was flat, eerie, as accusingly innocent as a child's.

"No, it's just Saturday night and I figured I'd drop in."

"Yeah, sure, okay."

She carved a space beside him on his musty floor amid the propped-open paperbacks and video clamshells and they watched his movie, as though repairing what Lucinda had neglected on her last visit, a full and earnest entry into Bedwin's universe. Lucinda drank straight from the bottle, while Bedwin fetched himself a beer from the refrigerator. Bedwin dimmed the lights, so the screen was the sole glow, blue patterns playing across their faces and curling around the bottle of scotch. The film's characters, confusingly, both worked on trains and rode as passengers on trains frequently in their spare time. It had a strange lulling rhythm, alternating between urgency and languor. The many looming shots of trains, tracks, and tunnels had a documentary authority that tended to dwarf the actors, one of whom was not Spencer Tracy, another not Marilyn Monroe. Lucinda detected Bedwin murmuring along very softly with the dialogue. Bedwin had allowed her inside a moment as pure and private as if she were watching him in sleep, digits jerking and eyelids trembling with a dream.

"Explain to me what you see in this," she said. "I really want to know."

"It's too much to explain."

"Just in this scene, then. Right now. What are you seeing?"

Bedwin turned his moonish face to her, surprisingly near. The blue screen stretched in miniature reflection in each of his lenses, the sun in a tiny solar system that also contained Lucinda's reflection and the space-capsule enclosure of Bedwin's book-lined room. Behind these teaspoon realms, she glimpsed his eyes: moist, large, feeble, and utterly unfamiliar.

"You really want to know?"

"Yes."

"Well, lately I've been focused on text fragments more than anything else," he said.

"Text fragments?"

"For instance, in the train yard, did you notice how they kept passing that sign that said 'Safety First—Think,' but the word 'Safety' was cut off so all you could see was 'fety'?"

"I think I did," she lied.

"It's as if the word itself had been wounded, the way a limb might get severed on a train track."

"I don't understand."

" 'Fety First—Think.' It's like an uncanny message from the unconscious of the film to the audience of 1954, telling them they live in a fundamentally unsafe reality."

"Wow."

"You can help me find more, if you want," he said hopefully.

"I'd love to."

"Watch this, this is an incredible one. On the wall of the bar, look. It says 'If You Don't See What You Want, Ask,' but the way the sign is formatted all you can read is 'You Don't See You Want,' which if you repunctuated it could be read as, 'You don't see, you *want*.' It's this total rebuke to the viewer's objectivity, the presumption that the audience can watch the behavior of the characters without becoming complicit in some way."

"My god, Bedwin, that's brilliant."

"I know, I know." He seemed not to be taking credit. Rather, the film's profundities had exfoliated themselves under his watch. And now hers as well.

"What about this one?" Lucinda said. "Look, it says 'Perfect Beer.'"

"Uh, you're right, it does."

"What do you think that's about?"

"I don't know, Lucinda, I guess that was just a brand of beer at the time that they were advertising in the bar."

"I know, but 'Perfect'? Doesn't that seem like they're at least slightly overstating the case?"

"Overstating which case?"

"What beer is perfect, right?"

"But it's not a fragment," said Bedwin. "The words are whole." His tone failed to mask disappointment.

"I'm sorry," she whispered, the scotch causing her to slur now.

"It's okay," he whispered back, ever suggestible.

"I'm just getting the feel."

"It's your first time," he said generously.

"You've opened my eyes."

Bedwin goggled behind his frames, flattered beyond speech. She lifted the glasses from his face and placed her forefinger alongside his nose, to smooth the ruddy gutter where the glasses had pressed his tender flesh, soothing him like a lobster for the slaughter. His lips parted. She kissed him. She hadn't lied. He'd opened her eyes, not to the insane excavation of text fragments from the movie about murderous train engineers but to Bedwin himself, his nobility and beauty. She ached to feel his precarious attention shifted entirely to the subject of her.

The band's secret genius was also Lucinda's, hiding in plain sight. It was Bedwin she loved, the answer to the question she'd only just formed. Wasn't he, after all, the true author of 'Monster Eyes,' before it had been poisoned by her with the complainer's lyrics? Bedwin lurked patiently, waiting to be recognized. If he watched her for a hundred or more times she'd reveal fragments he could painstakingly trace and study. Unlike Fritz Lang's film, she'd never be the same twice. In Bedwin she'd never inspire monster eyes, no. Someone so helpless could never discard her. As she kissed Bedwin and laughed and pulled him nearer to her she realized she'd be to him as Carl had been to her: enlivening, total, incomprehensible. Only she'd never abandon him, never quit her new life.

"Oh, wow, gosh, Lucinda," Bedwin breathed, from behind his panting return of her kisses, unwilling to stop but needing to register amazement.

"Yes, it's crazy, it's good."

"Wow, but I had no idea you felt—"

"I know, it's incredible we didn't think of it sooner."

"I guess—"

"Don't guess, there's nothing to guess." Lucinda covered him, tipped him. Bedwin's legs wriggled from beneath him and he and Lucinda fell enlaced, to occupy the oasis of carpet in Bedwin's vault, his snail shell. The film played in the background, urgent pensive voices under the soundtrack, *We weren't meant to be happy . . . it's always too late, isn't it? If only we'd been luckier, if something had happened to him in the yards . . .* Lucinda invaded Bedwin's T-shirt, palmed the knob of bone over his heart, the sprouts of hair defending his largish nipples. He licked and snuffled against her neck, supporting himself on his elbows, his fingertips gentle at her waist. She tugged her own blouse free.

"Lucinda?"

"Yes?"

"Can I ask you something?"

"Yes."

"Are you sleeping with Carl?"

"I was, but I'm not anymore."

"Oh. Can I ask you something else?"

"Yes, Bedwin, anything."

"Did Carl really write the lyrics to 'Monster Eyes' and those other songs?"

"Yes, Bedwin, he did. I mean, the parts that you didn't write or I didn't write."

"What parts did you write?"

"Just some of 'Monster Eyes,' I guess. Not the others. That was all you and Carl."

Bedwin's breath came in ragged shudders as Lucinda's hand ranged to his belly.

"Is it okay?"

"Yes," he managed. "It's just strange."

"This, you mean? Or collaborating with Carl?"

"Both."

She tried to smother his doubts on either subject, clambering so her unbound breasts swam onto his chest, whirling her tongue at his ear. She tore at the fly buttons of his jeans, which gave way easily.

"Luce—"

"Bed."

"Oh—"

She might have expected he'd be reticent, soft and afraid in his underwear, needing to be teased or beguiled. Instead he sprang into her palm, too ready, and all at once jetted soggily across her wrist.

"Oh, Bedwin," she said, astonished.

"Sorry."

"No, don't be sorry."

"I can't help it."

"There are ways—"

"No, not that. I mean I can't help being sorry."

Blue ghosts swam through the room. Lucinda blotted her wrist against Bedwin's shirt. He sighed his remorseful satisfaction, his spidery hands still idling at her waist. Lucinda lingered so early in her arc of arousal that any chance of reciprocity felt absurd. Bedwin stood as much chance of locating her desire now as of expertly piloting a steam shovel or minesweeper. She kissed the top of his head. He groped for his glasses, which were crushed beneath her hip. As he replaced them on his face he turned from her.

"I didn't know I meant anything to you," he said simply.

"Oh, Bedwin."

"I miss a lot of things. Stuff goes over my head."

"You're the smartest—"

"Listen to me. I'm shy. I'm not stupid. I can't meet people's eyes. I don't know if you understand what that's like. There's a whole world going on around me, I'm aware of that. It's not because I don't want to look at you, Lucinda. It's that I don't want to be seen. I'm afraid of what you'll see inside me. I'm ashamed, like you'll look in my eyes and see some kind of foul matter, something messed up."

"You're a beautiful man, Bedwin." Even as she spoke she understood they could never be together, that she'd come to him drunk on shame herself, reeling from the complainer's rejection. She saw Bedwin whole and real at last. Beautiful, in his way, he wasn't hers, had never been.

"I know there's a price for looking away," he said. "Everyone else is making stuff happen with their eyes. Connections, transactions. I don't know if you can understand how angry I feel sometimes."

"I'm sorry."

"It's not your fault. I just didn't know that you could see me. You always seemed a little, uh, frantic. I hope you don't mind my saying that."

"It's okay. I probably am frantic."

They were silent again, Bedwin straightening himself, rotating his head as if to shake water from his ear. Then he abruptly plunged to kiss her breasts, still bared in the blue gloom.

"Oh, Bedwin, no."

"What?"

"Just not now."

"Okay. Lucinda?"

"Yes?"

"What are we going to tell Denise?"

"What do you mean, tell Denise?"

"You know."

A horror fell on her at his words. She had every idea what Bedwin was talking about, all at once.

"I thought she just liked feeding you a lot of root beer and baloney sandwiches," she said.

"Ginger ale, Lucinda." A tone of hurt entered Bedwin's voice, as though this distinction was the world. Perhaps for him it was. It was just the sort of thing Denise would observe and attend to. Lucinda considered how a whole life, two lives, could be comprised of such gestures.

"Was there anything else between you?"

"Not technically, no."

"What do you mean, technically?"

"I mean, I guess I just always felt there was an understanding that we were sort of heading in a certain direction. There was you and Matthew—I mean, not anymore, I guess. But you can see how it seemed. The two very attractive and sort of flighty people had gotten together and the two somewhat more, uh, quiet and serious ones—"

"No, no, Bedwin—"

"Well, of course not now that we're, um—"

"No, Bedwin," she wailed. "Two people can't just drift toward each other so slowly, like glaciers, like continents, it's not fair to their friends—"

"I don't understand."

"I have to go, Bedwin."

"I love you, Lucinda."

"No, you don't," she said, though it was only what she'd told herself an hour earlier, less. "You don't, you don't."

For the second time that night she fled.


No complaints, no telephones, no band, no friends, no zoo, no kangaroo, no driving wildly to any other person's apartment, not even her own, none except that one to which he might return. No clothes, either, her garments were a false skin. She shed them as she moved across the floor to the bed, scattered them one by one until she pushed through his green curtain nude. No conversation this time, no false confrontations. She never wanted to know who Susan Ming was, should never have asked in the first place. She would only exist here in the complainer's bed until he returned.

He would. And find her. As he'd found her before, on the telephone, naked of anything but delight in him, expecting nothing. She'd return to that state. Had, in fact. And so waited, in the vast dark. Alone, consoled by the green curtain drawn around the smaller arena of the bed. The room was seamless to sound, a perfect rehearsal space, as it happened. Maybe all that had occurred to this point was only a kind of rehearsal. A demo tape. The band, her friends, her life. Now what mattered could begin. It was often this way, life consisted of a series of false beginnings, bluff declarations of arrival to destinations not even glimpsed. Seemingly permanent arrangements dissolved, stories piled up, exes amassed like old grievances. Always humorous in retrospect how important they'd seemed at the time. The little fiasco with Bedwin, for instance, already a legendary moment, rapidly receding into the past. Lucinda Hoekke was twenty-nine years old.

Spread on his comforter she made the attempt again to touch herself, inventorying what he'd had under his hands, what he'd nudged and lapped with his lips and tongue and blunt warm penis, all that she'd bared to him, now bared to the air and her own cool dry hands. What she'd given him was enough for anyone. She only had to have it ready here and not let the clutter of language rise up between the complainer and what she offered him—herself. She left herself unfiddled, unorgasmed, only triggered, tuned aware. In the perfect silence and the imperfect dark, night-lit clouds passing in pale drawn reflection on the white ceiling. She waited, closed her eyes, limbs buzzing with readiness. Parted lips. Imagined him returned. Soon enough snored.

The voices came to her, what seemed just instants later, in a dream of the loft flooded with orange sunlight, toasting her brain through shuttered eyelids. She basked in this light without opening her eyes, smiled and arched her back, kept from breaking the spell of her half slumber, not sure why the dream should please her so much as it did. It involved two people she adored, two members of Monster Eyes, her band.

"I appreciate your making the time to meet with me on such short notice."

"Sure, buddy, why wouldn't I?"

"This sort of thing is extremely difficult for me."

"Do you want something to drink?"

"No, thank you."

"Sorry, this place is a wreck. I've got to get someone in here to clean it up."

"I don't mind. It was very generous of you to let us rehearse here all those times."

"Cripes, Bedwin. I was in the band then, remember? Quit thanking me for everything, you're making me nervous. It's like the buildup to some kind of accusation."

"I don't blame you for anything."

"That's a relief. I'm going to make some coffee. This is pretty early by my lights. Sure you don't want any?"

"No, thanks. I've been up for hours. Anyway, I'm awfully sensitive to caffeine."

"Me too, why else drink it? Pull up a chair, tell me what's on your mind."

"I need to talk to you about the songs."

"What about them?"

"Now that we're not working together, I figured we should address the, uh, situation of our sort of semi-voluntary collaboration, so we can find some way to resolve things and move forward."

"This was your idea, or someone put you up to it?"

"Mine and Denise's."

"What about the rest of the band?"

"Actually, there is no more band."

"That was sudden."

"It happened last night."

"What happened?"

"It's not going to be possible for the band to go on from this point. I can't explain any better than that."

"Fair enough. I don't need an explanation. What's the scheme with the songs?"

In this uncannily exact and extensive dream Lucinda now heard the whirling racket of coffee beans in a miniature grinder, the tap-tap of the grind being emptied into the espresso machine's strainer.

"Denise and I may continue with our musical project under another name. Several of the songs I'd like to go on playing. As I told you, I find this very awkward."

"I get it. This is like a divorce settlement. What I can't understand is why Denise didn't come too."

"She's a little upset about this whole thing. Anyway, as I understand it the songs belong to you and me, no one else."

"I guess that's right."

"I don't want you to feel that Denise and I want nothing more to do with you from here on, but I think it's important that I leave here today with this matter clarified one way or the other between us, so that no other, uh, parties will be able to, uh, exploit any ambiguities, if you know what I mean."

"It's a fascinating problem. Really, you could slice it a dozen different ways."

"You should probably tell me what you have in mind."

"For instance, we could just divvy them up, you get some, I get some. Or we could split them down the middle, lyrics and music. Take out what we came in with, right? Only, what good does that do anyone? Maybe we should split them the other way, you take the words, me the tunes. That way we've each got what we didn't have before. You're good at music, you can write new melodies. I can easily think up some more slogans for your songs. Let a thousand flowers bloom."

"That's an odd thought."

"Or there's the option of a nihilistic conflagration. We can declare the songs dead to either one of us."

"However awkward, this collaboration represents a significant chapter in my creative life."

"Well, that sinks it, then, I'd say. You sure you don't want some of this coffee? It came out perfect."

"If you had some orange juice, I'd have that."

"Better yet, I've got a bag of oranges, we'll squeeze some. Just let me wash off a chopping block. What a sty. You want some toast or something?"

"Sure. What do you mean 'that sinks it'?"

"Well, despite collaborating on those songs, Bedwin, you're

looking at someone without a creative life, let alone one with significant chapters. The whole line of thinking is pretty exotic to me."

"So you're going to keep the songs just because you've never created anything of value to anyone before?"

"You don't pull any punches, do you? Here, hand me that pitcher."

"It's full of crushed limes."

"Maybe give it a quick rinse."

"I didn't mean to sound hostile." Water ran, dishes clanked, the toaster's coils clicked: the two were making breakfast together. "You have to excuse me, I'm no good at this kind of thing. I just can't help wondering what value the songs have to you."

"That's the point I was trying to make."

"Sorry?"

"You should help yourself. Take them outright, no charge."

"Really?"

"Sure. If they mean that much to you. Truth is, I was never so into music in the first place. You know, I've got some bacon and eggs in here, it really wouldn't be hard to put together a little fry-up."

"That sounds good, actually."

"Nobody doesn't like a fry-up."

Now the dream had become richly olfactory, and following on the scent of coffee and toast came fumes of sizzling bacon grease and butter.

"So if you were to, say, hear the song 'Monster Eyes' on the radio, even if it became, say, hugely popular and a sort of contemporary classic, you'd have no problem with that, we could expect nothing in the way of regrets or recriminations from you at any point in the future?"

"Nope."

"There's nothing you want in return?"

"Well, I was wondering if you and Denise already had a singer in mind." There was an interval of silence before he spoke again. "Just kidding."

"Oh."

"But I'm curious—who's handling the vocals?"

"Denise says I have a very expressive voice, I just have to trust it."

"That's great. Here, pass me that pepper. Actually, if you would, just keep this from sticking. That's the way, move it gently from the edges of the pan."

"I'm not much of a cook."

"It's coming along nicely. I like my eggs wet, in fact."

Their talk was punctuated by the clank of silverware now, and by the sighs and smacks of hearty chewing. Lucinda idled, naked and unseen behind the green curtain, still in reverie. So long as she remained silent and selfless the two players were essentially as she preferred them: benign, enchanted, fond.

"I just realized I recognize those clothes on the floor."

"I do apologize for the mess."

"No, but I mean specifically those are Lucinda's clothes."

"She left a lot of stuff lying around here. She pretty much moved in for a while. But you knew that."

"But what I'm trying to say is those are specifically exactly the clothes Lucinda wore last night, quite late last night in fact. I happen to be absolutely certain."

"You could be right."

"She's awful."

"She's just a mixed-up person, Bedwin."

"You're entitled to your opinion, but I think Lucinda is a genuinely reprehensible person."

"That's why it's no go with the band, huh?"

"I never want to see her again. I can't even stand to look at those clothes."

"We'll just throw them in the garbage, then. Have to get this whole place swept out, but it's a start."

"There's more, over there. Her underwear."

"Holy smoke, it's everywhere, you're right."

"Should we light it on fire?"

"That's a little dramatic, don't you think?"

"I suppose."

"Just push it down in there with the eggshells."

"Ugh, okay, there."

No dream. Lucinda's sick eyes opened to the blaze of day to which she lay bare, her lips and nipples and the microscopic hairs of her stomach and thighs alive to tiny breezes, her breath cinched in anxiety. She might pull the bedspread to cover herself or insert her body within the layers of sheet but feared rustling, giving herself away to what now seemed enemies. Bedwin and the complainer clanked plates in trickling water, noises that made proof she was alive and only a few feet from the kitchen where the two had been eating and talking.

"Just scrape the plate, I'll do the dishes later."

"Thanks for the meal and everything, I mean for being so understanding about the songs."

"They're your songs, Bedwin."

"Well, thank you."

"Never speak of it again."

"Okay. See you later."

"Sure, see you later, except honestly you probably won't, if I get the drift of things."

"Honestly, I expect that's true."

"Hold on a second and I'll go down in the elevator with you. This place actually depresses me a little bit right now, I don't want to be alone here."

They were gone. Silence reigned, the impossible morning restored to her alone. She crept from behind the curtain. Her clothes had been collected and ruined in the tall chrome garbage pail, layered into a compost of char and bacon grease, eggshells, coffee grounds, rinds of squeezed oranges and bloated, soaking limes. If she retrieved the clothes she'd be wearing breakfast. She didn't want them anyway, they'd been polluted by hate as much as by garbage. To fetch them would confess that she'd been concealed, that she'd heard what she'd heard. She wormed one hand in and found the pocket of her jeans, seized her keys and a few balled dollars. Her forearm emerged speckled with oil-dark grounds, which she swept back into the mass.

She wouldn't wear his clothes for a thousand reasons. Too huge for her, she'd be garbed in the costume of a hobo clown. Better go naked to her car than that. She thought of stripping the green curtain from his bed, sweeping her way to the elevator and out draped royally in velvet. But no souvenirs, not today. There was just one thing in this place that no longer belonged to the complainer, besides herself. Falmouth's drawings, the record of the band's rehearsals. She undraped the enormous pad's pages from where they lay across the pinball machine, rolled them into a neat tube which she pinned beneath her armpits. The cone of pages made a rigid dress planing from ribs to knees, a child's drawing come to life. Falmouth would have been proud. Barefoot, clutching keys, elbows pinned to ribs, she managed an exit garbed in the cone, down the elevator alone, out into the vacant glare of morning. Nobody saw her wriggle into her Datsun, half nude. The drawings went into the backseat. Falmouth's charcoal, never set with any fixative, had impressed a faint record of the inmost of the drawings on her moist hips and belly, a hieroglyphic procession of smudged figures. She rubbed these off easily, raising a slight pinkness on her flesh, then drove home, eyes set straight ahead on the freeway, oblivious to gawkers, bare of clothing, drawings, or any other thing she'd ever imagined could conceal her.

# six

the porpoises arced from the wave tops parallel to the beach, just yards from where the surf itched and boiled at the sun-bright sand. Equidistant, and rotating like targets in an arcade as if mounted on cogs beneath the line of the water, the animals kept silent time with the walkers on the beach, seeming apart, hallucinated, ethereal, embodying heedless liberty despite their almost military precision. The porpoises might seem to have come to welcome and escort the sand-walkers, the gulpers of gullet-warming scotch from a bottle they'd left behind in a nook in the rocks, the intoxicated lovers who explored El Matador Beach, a site of nearly catastrophic beauty only twenty-five minutes from the baked interior west of La Cienega on which they ordinarily mapped their whole lives.

El Matador's sand was littered with ragged geologic forms, pylons and archways of stone scoured by salt-bearing wind. The sky made a blue forgiving table over the sand's glare, which was impossible to face directly, as though the lovers fire-walked the sun's surface itself. Pale humans, they felt their vanities smashed in this collision of water, stone, and sky, so the sea creatures turning like pinwheels struck a note of mammalian solidarity, a solace. But no, it was a lie. The walkers subtly sped up to keep time, but the porpoises' indifference was soon made plain. In their easy looping they swam twice as fast as the walkers advanced, escorting no one. Then they were gone, try as you might to locate them again in the glistening expanse. The lovers were alone again in this place, together.

"I concede the fact that this beach exists and has always existed outside of us but right now it feels to me like this is our emotional landscape made real. If you could read the meaning of the insane shape of those cliffs and pillars you'd know everything I feel about you."

"It's like a giant heart or a brain we're walking inside, though maybe I'm drunk. I feel like those gulls are watching us now."

"People are psychedelic to each other, under ideal conditions."

"Who said that?"

"Nobody, I mean, I did, just now."

"I can't believe we never came here. Who told you about this place?"

"Falmouth. He said he was sick of looking at me, I was too happy. He said he'd pay me for the day if we followed his exact instructions, to drive up the coast and ignore all the beaches until we got to El Matador. We're supposed to eat at Neptune's Net, too, a fish shack farther up the highway. You have to admit he has some good ideas."

"He has a lot of good ideas."

"Matthew?"

"What?"

"Why do you never get jealous?"

"I do get jealous."

"Tell me what you love about me."

"Everything."

"No, come on, something specific."

"I love most of all your wild integrity."

"What's that supposed to mean?"

They'd been reunited for two or three days, depending how you counted, a dizzy sleepless binge. Two weeks had passed since the Monday morning Lucinda delivered the unruined drawings to the storefront gallery and presented them to Falmouth. Falmouth, rousing himself, had hired Lucinda to supervise matting and framing the charcoal-on-paper artworks in archival settings. His show opened in another month, under the title "Monster Eyes: Disband." Falmouth had totally repoised himself, shaved the stubble that had briefly revealed him as not bald, only balding. These days he was usually talking on the phone or squinting at his computer, waving Lucinda through, letting chicken-salad sandwiches stiffen on rafts of wax paper on his desk, too busy for lunch. The opening's after party would be thrown by Jules Harvey.

Denise and Bedwin had absconded, like Bonnie and Clyde,

into their universe of baloney and ginger ale. There had been no further bargaining or recrimination, the songs were taken, gone, theirs. One morning a few scraps of equipment, microphones, stands, cable, had been delivered anonymously to Falmouth's storefront. These belonged rightfully to Matthew; his zoo income had been their stake when the four had formed the band. Two days later Lucinda opened the *Echo Park Annoyance* to find a notice among the music listings, billing the defectors' first gig, at Spaceland, opening for the Rain Injuries. *Urban and Greenish, acoustic duo, formerly of Monster Eyes.*

Lucinda nudged Matthew back to the sandy nook where they'd half buried the bottle of Oban. She tripped him, stuck her ankle between his and shoved his skinny frame down to the moist shaded sand. He leaned on his elbows and they both sipped from the bottle. Lucinda unbuttoned his jeans and nibbled the tiny procession of hairs, so scant it was like punctuation, stray commas and parentheses, trailing to the coils below. He wore no underwear. El Matador was too public, but she cooled him in her mouth for just a moment, a promise for later. Matthew's head lolled, his throat's knuckle to the sky. His substance throbbed, so real and hot, smoother than her numb chappy lips. His narrow pelvis barely filled his jeans. His elegant scrawny limbs, so familiar and unfamiliar at once. Everything between them was new and right. Matthew tugged his jeans over himself and they fled the shaded cranny and scrambled back through the beach's maze of forms and up the ice plant–ridged knoll to where they'd left Matthew's Mazda.

Neptune's Net was another revelation, as grand and strange as the name suggested. Its broad eating porch overlooked the coastal highway and beyond, to the waves dotted with surfers bobbing like floes. The restaurant was a secret destination only to them, mobbed by eaters: middle-aged valley couples, tanned Malibu executives, feral bands of teens, Asian families like strings of ducklings, bikers in chaps, anyone but hipsters, the vast galaxy of anyone who'd never in a million years attend Jules Harvey's parties, a vision as humbling in its way as the indifferent sea and sky. They chowed in pure animal bliss, at long picnic tables strewn with carapaces of shrimp, crab, and lobster, oil-stained paper trays of fried scallops and clams, french fries, squeezed sleeves of ketchup and tartar, drained bottles of Corona and Zima. Matthew and Lucinda placed an order at the counter, lobster and shrimp, then took their numbered token and went to pick beers from a back room loaded with glass-fronted coolers.

"Sapporo," said Lucinda, pointing at the tall silver canister that had drawn her eye.

They sat waiting at the edge of the porch, sharing a picnic table with a large woman in a lime pantsuit with a tiny dog. She sat alone over a lobster and a tray of fries, her leashed pet coursing at her ankles. Matthew and Lucinda gazed over the highway, where convertibles slid to destinations even less imaginable than this one, Big Sur, Baja, Alaska. The restaurant's loudspeaker crackled out numbers, so loud they echoed off the cliffs above, never theirs. Matthew and Lucinda felt at the exact edge of their lives, feeling them close, closer, as near at hand and yet elusive as the wind that whistled in their hair: the true complete lives in which they would at last drown, the oceanic voyage into their thirties and beyond, through which their inchoate yearnings would be either soothed or disappointed, or both.

Somehow, Lucinda knew, they'd be famous. When they were it would be funny to say that they had once been in a band. The fantasy expanded: Urban and Greenish would be famous too, and it would be lovely and funny that they had been in a band together, when they were younger. Those who admired their work would see it as a measure of the inevitability of their fame, that they were all once in the same band. Lucinda drained at her Sapporo, pleased by its seeming bottomlessness, its cool buzz thrilling her blood like a higher form of oxygen. Would she and Matthew be together forever or would it later only be funny or odd that they had once been in a band together too? But this was nonsense, a glitch in her mood. She and Matthew belonged together. It was only astonishing they'd wasted so much time not seeing what was likely obvious to others. Certainly Falmouth had known, though he'd been too wise to press her. He'd given them a gift, a sort of unofficial wedding present, by commanding them to visit this place. In his way, Falmouth was a romantic. Lucinda loved him, too.

The pantsuited woman's tiny dog barked cyclically at his master's discarded lobster shell, thinking it had discovered a villain. The woman heaved a sigh and asked Matthew and Lucinda if they would guard her seat and her food while she locked the dog in the car. They agreed, then without consultation pillaged the mound of fries the moment the woman was out of sight of the porch.

It was at that moment a bicycle built for two rounded the curve of highway, laboring northward to ascend the ridge on which Neptune's Net perched. Two figures of substance, dressed absurdly in black sunglasses, baggy sweatpants clipped at the ankles, and white rubber-soled shoes resembling a nurse's, teetering on the elaborate bicycle's wobbling tires, knees trembling with the effort of depressing the pedals. Dr. Marian in the rear seat, the complainer in front, both their ruddy faces shining with sweat. They looked immutably right together, a symbiotic unit. Dr. Marian leaned forward in her seat, her expression fierce as she whispered in the complainer's ear, incanting him forward. She worked too, resolutely fair, her powerful thighs driving downward in coordination with his. The complainer's expression was grim, his mouth set, eyes helpless, yet his bearing conveyed some measure of inner placidity Lucinda had never glimpsed. The tandem bicycle reached the top and the riders' struggle eased. They began to coast, their backdrop the first blush of a pale distant sunset.

The complainer wore a T-shirt reading NOBODY KNOWS I'M SUICIDAL.

"Look," Lucinda said.

"Is that—"

"Shhh, just let them pass."

The riders were soon gone beyond the curve of highway, off toward who knew what. Perhaps merely a different fish shack, higher up the coast. Lucinda was glad they'd appeared. It was another harbinger of happiness for herself and Matthew, but she felt glad too that the couple had passed without detecting their audience at the porch rail.

"Does he ever come around the zoo office?"

"A couple of times."

"Do you talk?"

Matthew shrugged. "He's a very friendly guy."

Lucinda decided not to ask more. "It's strange to think about now," she said.

The large woman returned without her dog. Matthew and Lucinda daubed guiltily at the greasy corners of their mouths and scooted away from her fries.

"What's strange to think about?" said Matthew.

"The whole thing." Lucinda stopped herself. "I mean, that he was actually in the band."

"There's something I never told you."

"What's that?"

"At certain times I felt like Carl was the only real artist out of all of us," said Matthew. "I mean, I suppose this is kind of crazy, but he reminded me of Elvis Presley, like he was some kind of idiot savant trying to invent something new, to break through to a new kind of sound."

"It's possible, I guess."

"Okay, it's ridiculous."

"Yes."

"It's totally ridiculous."

Lucinda was done with this part of the conversation. "You know what I love most about you?" she asked.

"What?"

She grabbed his arm, grabbed his neck, pulled him to her, whispered against his bristly sinewy cheek. She felt so hungry she almost wanted to take a bite. Neptune's Net would call their number soon. "The way the veins in your forearms stick out. And the ridge of muscle that runs along your waist. I love that you're skinny."

"That's superficial, Lucinda."

"You can't be deep without a surface."

—fin—

# Acknowledgments

Special thanks to Amy Greenstadt, for help inventing this story. Thanks also Pamela Jackson, Will Amato, Diane Martel, Alice Eckles, Maureen Linker, Alexis Rivera, Kat Silverstein, Philip Price, Heidi Julavits, Rodrigo Fresán, Rebecca Donner, Lauren Mechling, Sean Howe, Andrew Hultkrans, Chris Sorrentino, Bill, Richard, Amy.